Dungeon Crawlers

Episode 1

STEFAN U.G. LEBLANC

TIAC Communications

Copryright © 2010 by Stefan U.G. LeBlanc

Published by TIAC Communications

Books published by TIAC Communications are available at special discounts for bulk purchases by corporations, institutions, and other organizations. For more information visit our website http://www.tiaccommunications.com or email info@tiaccommunications.com.

Canadian Cataloging in Publication Data
Stefan U.G. LeBlanc, 1989 -
Dungeon Crawlers Episode 1

A CIP catalog record for this book is available from Library and Archives Canada

ISBN: 1-896780-03-2

Stefan Ulric Gary LeBlanc

Stefan Ulric Gary LeBlanc was born October 2, 1989 in Vancouver, British Columbia Canada. He attended the University of California Los Angeles Acting and Performance Institute and is presently an undergraduate student at Butler University, Indianapolis, Indiana, awarded an auditioned talent scholarship by the Jordan College of Fine Arts. Stefan is majoring in theater, minoring in Spanish, and continues his creative passions writing screenplays, plays, adventures for role playing games, short stories, and the Dungeon Crawlers saga, a science fiction fantasy epic of adventure and intrigue.

Having a remarkable breadth of life experiences at a young age, acting and writing his first short story at age four, Stefan has represented Canada at the United Nations Environment Programme International Children's Conference on the Environment at age twelve and was a young leader with a Canada World Youth Latin America international programme for six months at age seventeen. Stefan was also invited to attend the inaugural Ignite Change Now-Global Youth Assembly 2009 presented by the John Humphrey Centre for Peace and Human Rights together with the Canadian Commission for UNESCO designed to connect youth and young professionals across Canada and the world.

Stefan wants to contribute to the world, to make a positive impact, and to bring joy to his audiences. His well-developed sense of humor and understanding of human nature allows him to bring his memorable characters to life.

Dungeon Crawlers

The strong gusts of wind assaulted Lars Nokuten's bright red hair as he surveyed the fortress ahead of him. He could see various military vehicles and equipment waiting to be used at the slightest possible hint of an intruder. Fortunately, the Steel Falcon was significantly out of sight and several thousand feet in the air. The sky ship was old but it contained a lot of memories for Lars, and he wouldn't trade it for all the world. He grinned as he heard footsteps approach him from behind.

"Izlude! Are we ready for our siege?" Lars said with a chuckle.

"...How did you know it was me?" Izlude responded in shock.

"After all the time we've spent together, you don't think I'd know your footsteps?" Lars said as he turned around to face him.

"Marina and the others...they seem really on edge." Izlude said, glancing to his left.

"On edge? What's there to be on edge about? We're only going to take a rusty, old, tin can of a sky ship into a highly-guarded military base with a handful of people on our side, and a thousand of highly-trained military personnel on theirs." Lars replied with a grin. "Don't sweat it, Izlude. We've been in tighter spots before. What would your mother say? She ran head-first into trouble without so much as a second thought."

A large explosion rocked the ship, jostling the two severely. Lars grasped tightly onto a nearby railing with one hand and held onto Izlude with the other.

"...I think they spotted us, Lars." Izlude stammered.

"Nah, they couldn't have. It's prolly just Tekky working on another experiment. You remember the last time-" Lars was cut off as another explosion, more severe than the last, rocked the ship more.

"Uh...yeah...I definitely think they've spotted us." Izlude said with a cough as he inhaled some smoke.

"Sir! Heavy damage to the starboard side! It missed knocking off the wing by a few feet!" a familiar girl shouted, running towards the pair.

"Izlude, Marina! You know what this means?" Lars said as he lowered his head slightly, shadows covering his green eyes.

"What does it mean...?" Izlude nervously asked while Marina placed a hand on Lars' shoulder.

"It means I'm royally ticked off! Get Tekky to fire up the engines, make sure the cannons are ready to be fired! We're gonna have a little fun!" Lars said, pointing his broadsword to the heavens and grinning.

CHAPTER 1

The night was unusually chilly as Izlude crouched behind the Warthog Pub. His light brown hair blustered furiously in protest against his pale forehead. He glanced around nervously, cringing as the trees cast moving shadows across his path. If the village chief caught them now, they'd be thrown in the lake with rocks tied to their ankles for sure. Izlude wasn't entirely sure why he had let his brother convince him to act as a scout while he and his band of friends, the self-proclaimed Mercenaries, looted the village pub's alcohol supply. Not only was it stealing, normally punished by banishment, but also almost all of them were underage. Izlude had just turned fifteen a couple of weeks ago, and his brother Lars was the only one legal at the age of twenty-one.

"But, bro! I...isn't that illegal?" Izlude had stammered.

"Aw, grow a backbone! It's only semi-illegal, and besides, how's that fat, old man they call the chief going to catch us?" Lars had laughed as he clapped a hand on Izlude's smaller shoulder, his green eyes shining in the sunlight.

"But we could get banished and then eaten by monsters...or killed for sport by the sky pirates...or even drafted into the Lucarian Empire's army!" Izlude had protested greatly.

"We should be so lucky, damn it! All of those things are more interesting than wasting our lives away in this small village! All we do day in and day out is farm!" Lars had said with a large grin.

Izlude couldn't counter this with anything logical, so he reluctantly let Lars include him in this plan, the days following included nervousness, paranoia, and sleepless nights for Izlude. Most times he simply listened to Lars' snoring. Izlude often thought about where he came from during sleepless nights. He couldn't remember their parents. Lars had told him that they had died in a barn fire when he was still a baby.

A sudden crash came from the inside of the pub. Izlude was shaken from his thoughts and snapped back to reality. He whipped his head around looking for anything, or worse, anyone who could have made the noise. People had been mysteriously disappearing from the village at night, and this was the last place he wanted to be. He slowly made his way around to the front of the pub, its brick walls brushed against his skin uncomfortably. Izlude tapped the front door and watched it start to open inwards. He quickly flattened himself against the wall beside it and shut his eyes.

"It's okay...everything's okay. I'm going to go inside, and there's going to be nobody but Lars and the others." Izlude spoke out loud to himself with his eyes closed.

Izlude took in a deep breath and threw himself inside. The darkness greeted him and even the light of the moon couldn't penetrate inside the pub. Izlude stumbled on an over-turned chair but managed to catch himself before falling down completely. A loud, familiar voice destroyed the silence and Izlude approached the direction.

"Well way to go! 'I never get to hold the torch, why can't I hold the torch?' my butt!" shouted the voice of Kilik, a member of the Mercenaries.

"It could've been worse. We're inside a pub with a wooden interior and lots of alcohol around, do the math." replied Grerr.

"I never was good at math, that doesn't sound like it adds up all too well. But, we push on!" Lars said as he walked forward.

"But how will we know which way to go? We don't have any light thanks to Mr. Smooth as Sandpaper here." muttered Kilik.

"Will you cut me some slack?!" yelled Nak from the ground.

"Yeah, cut him some slack, let's just check out...sorry there Nak..." Lars said while accidentally stepping on top of Nak and remaining there, "this direction over here. Besides, we didn't know where to look with the light anyways."

"But what if the chief comes and finds us? We'll be in

serious trouble. I say we should quit while we're ahead. We already have a couple of bottles, right guys?" Grerr suggested.

"Had. Clumsy feet there shattered the two of them." Kilik sighed.

"Well what do you expect having me carry three things like that? And will you please get off of me, Lars?!" Nak groaned.

"Well, it's only water under the...er...whatever the water goes under. Besides, the chief's not going to catch us! No one knows we're even in here!" Lars shouted triumphantly, ignoring Nak.

"Hey...bro? Is everything-" Izlude began to speak.

"Holy-!" Lars yelled as he jumped backwards, forgetting that only moments earlier he had been standing on top of Nak, and crashed to the floor with a loud bang.

"Sorry, bro, I didn't mean to scare you like that." Izlude apologized.

"You didn't scare me! You startled me. There's a difference, right guys?" Lars insisted as he picked himself up off the ground.

A flash of bright light illuminated the room temporarily from further inside the pub and then slowly dimmed. Lars turned in its direction and squinted.

"Hey, Lars...I think there's someone else in here with us." Kilik whispered.

"C'mon, let's check out where that flash came from, unless you're too 'startled', Lars." Grerr jabbed.

"Hah! I'm not scared of anything! Gimme a sec and I'll make us another torch. I swear, we wouldn't have these problems if Drom wasn't so secluded from the outer world's technology. I mean, if technology was good enough for the Arcanians, why is our chief so against humanity reverse-engineering it? Heck, we ship off our food using sky ships." Lars muttered to no one in particular, ripping off a piece of his shirt and stuffing it inside a nearby bottle.

The room was suddenly visible again once Lars lit the end of the alcohol-soaked cloth. He grinned and motioned for the five of them to continue towards the back room where the light had come from. After stepping over the damaged stools and chair, their small party arrived in what appeared to be a library.

"What could a bartender ever want with a library?" Kilik asked as he picked up a random book.

"Search me. Maybe he liked reading?" Nak offered his suggestion.

"Gee, ya think?" replied Kilik, his voice dripping in sarcasm.

"Something's not quite right here, Lars." Grerr said as he examined a particular bookcase.

Lars approached him from behind and held his makeshift torch in front of where Grerr was looking. The flames immediately blew away from the bookcase, and Lars had to cup his hand in front of the flames to stop them from going out completely. Izlude slowly made his way over to his brother and Grerr and also looked at the bookcase.

"I think maybe there's a hidden passage behind this. There appears to be quite a draft coming from it." Grerr speculated.

"...Maybe you have to take a certain book out?" Izlude suggested.

"Do you have any idea how many books are here? We could be pulling these out until doomsday!" Lars exclaimed. "We'll just let our brawn take care of it, right Kilik?"

"I think I resent that." Kilik said while pushing on the side of the bookcase with great effort.

Kilik kept struggling with the wooden bookcase and it wasn't until he slipped and fell face forward that he exclaimed that he was giving up.

"Who's clumsy now?" laughed Nak, satisfied.

"Well now what? Start grabbing random books?" Lars asked as he leaned against the bookcase.

"Hey, this book looks kind of odd...it's multi-colored." Izlude said about a book he had just removed from the bookcase.

"Well, it obviously can't be that one, Izlude. It's way too...obvious!" Grerr said as he shook his head.

A bright flash filled the room and the bookcase quickly slid backwards, revealing a dark passageway and steps going down.

"Whoa!" Lars yelled as he fell backwards for the second time that night and slid on his back down the stairs and into the darkness.

"Well...there goes our torch again." muttered Kilik.

"Heck with the torch! There goes Lars!" yelled Grerr as he ran after him.

"Bro, are you okay?!" Izlude shouted.

Izlude plunged into the darkness with Grerr, leaving Nak and Kilik in the library by themselves.

"I can either stay here and waste Goddess knows how long talking to you, or go into the darkness, have an accident and probably bleed to death. Tough choice." Kilik sighed as he entered the passageway.

Seeing he was alone, Nak quickly ran behind him.

Lars groaned as he knelt on the ground and picked up his source of light. A small crack had formed on the bottom of the bottle and a few drops of alcohol were dripping out, but nothing too serious. A hand grabbed Lars on the shoulder causing him to yell.

"Take it easy, Lars! It's me, Grerr!" Grerr ducked a punch from Lars.

"Thought you were a monster." Lars explained as he scratched the back of his head.

"You okay, bro? That fall looked kind of...nasty." Izlude asked, concerned.

"Hah, you think a fall like that's gonna hurt me? I meant to do that!" Lars said as he struck a heroic pose. "Get your butts in gear! Let's check out this passageway."

Kilik and Nak quickly caught up and the five of them marched down the musty hallway at the bottom of the stairs. Surrounding them were rough, stone edges that protruded at strange angles. The sand floor was filled with puddles that microscopically increased every few seconds by the odd drips from the ceiling. A sudden roar caused Lars, Izlude and the others to pause in their tracks.

"...Did you hear that?" Izlude asked, his voice quivering.

"Yeah, just the wind, that's all." Lars coughed.

A loud scream filled the halls only seconds later, causing the five to slowly take a few steps backwards.

"Since when does wind scream?" Kilik questioned Lars' response.

"Since now, apparently." Lars scratched the back of his head, "Let's check it out!"

"Are you insane?!" Grerr yelled as Lars sprinted towards the source.

"Well, now what?" Nak asked without taking his eyes off Lars running away with their only source of light.

"We can't let him go off on his own, c'mon guys! He'd do the same for you!" Grerr exclaimed as he grabbed onto Izlude and the two of them ran after Lars.

"Why am I always stuck with you?" Kilik turned to Nak and asked.

The four eventually caught up to Lars who was crouched on the ground over a freshly slain body. It had deep claw marks slashed all across it, and blood had seeped into the sand. A metallic broadsword was still in the body's right hand.

"Is he dead, bro?!" Izlude gagged.

"Nah, he's just taking a breather. Of course he's dead, moron!" Kilik shouted.

"Hey! Don't talk to Izlude like that! Save it for Nak." Lars said as he stood up to face them.

"What do you mean by that?!" Nak protested.

Another roar echoed through the room they were in and it was much louder than before. Lars cautiously raised his makeshift torch in its direction. The light travelled along the right-hand wall before revealing a corner and a hulking shadow of something that was breathing heavily.

"What did you mean about not letting him go off on his own?" Kilik whispered to Grerr.

"I think we've overstayed our welcome, guys...let's just get out of here..." Lars whispered quietly.

The shadow took a few steps forwards and eventually stood in full view of the party. A large, striped creature extended its claws and roared once again, showing a full set of jagged teeth. Its two muscular legs bulged as it did so. The five boys screamed and Lars did the only thing he could think of. He threw his torch at the monster. The bottle shattered on it and the creature roared in agony as the flames caught on its fur and began melting it in front of them. It swiftly turned around and ran deeper into the passageway.

Silence filled the room.

"Well, that was gruesome." Lars said.

CHAPTER 2

"Right. Sorry, Lars. That's where I draw the line. Count me out." Kilik shouted as he sprinted back the way they came.

"Wait for me, Kilik! I'm right behind you!" Nak yelled as he ran behind him in terror.

"You cowards!" Lars shouted after them. "Geez, they see one tiny monster and they run."

"That monster wasn't tiny, bro..." Izlude muttered as he silently pleaded for Lars to tell him that their adventure was over.

"Well, now what're we going to do?" Grerr asked, unusually calm as always.

"What're we going to do? We're going to kill that thing!" Lars stated as he bent down and felt around the body at his feet.

"Simple as that? 'We're going to kill that thing'? And how do you suppose we do that? Look at what happened to...well...whoever that was." Grerr argued.

"Well," Lars said as he found a flashlight hidden on the body and clicked it on, "...I love technology ...first of all, that thing could go around and kill people. Now, if I could rig it so that it only killed the chief, I'd let it live. Since I can't do that, we're going to have to just take care of it ourselves."

"No way! We can't do that! It'd be dangerous!" Izlude protested.

"The monster *did* look pretty weakened from being burned that badly." Grerr thought out loud.

"You can't be thinking about urging him to do this, Grerr!" Izlude cried out as he grabbed onto his brother.

A sickening crunch answered Izlude as Lars ripped the broadsword out of the unknown man's hand. Lars scrutinized it closer under the light.

"What? 'lahG sivraJ ot sgnoleb drows sihT?' " Lars struggled to pronounce the strange sentence in front of him.

"You read it backwards, Lars. You're holding it upside-down." Grerr reprimanded as he flipped the broadsword around for him.

"Right, I knew that. 'This sword belongs to Jarvis Ghal'...the bartender? What the heck was he doing down here?" Lars pondered to himself.

"We need to go back and explain this to the chief! We could get blamed for it! We shouldn't be down here, bro!" Izlude stammered.

"C'mon, Izlude! Where's your sense of adventure?" Lars chuckled.

"It left with Nak and Kilik! Now let's go!" Izlude yelled, desperately trying to pull Lars back towards the stairs.

"Even though the chief can be pretty blind about things, I don't think he'll look at the claw marks on Jarvis' body and think, 'It had to have been Lars, Izlude, and Grerr!!' " he said as he motioned with the broadsword towards the poor man's body.

"We don't even know which way it went! These tunnels must be linked together like ant tunnels!" Izlude exclaimed as he finally started to give in to Lars' half-baked idea.

"I think we might find it if we follow the trail it's left us." Grerr said, pointing at something shimmering on the sandy floor.

"Well, what do you know?" Lars mused as he shined his new-found flashlight on the floor, "That thing bleeds! C'mon, let's follow it."

The three slowly followed the trail taking lefts and rights as required until a soft roar entered their ears. Izlude threw himself in front of Lars and held his arms out to block him.

"Wait! Do you hear that? The monster's really upset about something!" Izlude yelled.

"Nah, that can't be the monster, either that or he doesn't need to breathe, because that sound has been going on for a good minute now." Lars said after listening to it for a while.

The roaring got slowly louder and louder as they walked further down the hallway. The hallway seemed to open up into a dimly lit cavern. Lars casually strode in with Izlude walking cautiously behind him, glancing every now and then at the walls around them. A few steps further, the trail appeared to end. A dozen feet below them was a running stream.

"Damn, the trail ends." Lars said with a shake of his head.

"Maybe he backtracked? Went the wrong way by accident?" Grerr sighed as he picked up a rock and tossed it into the stream.

"Wait, that's it! The monster was on fire, right?" Lars shouted, full of excitement as he ran to the edge. "So that means he wanted to extinguish the flames, right?"

"What's your point here, Lars?" Grerr replied as he sat on the ground and sighed some more.

"My point is that it must have jumped into the stream here to cool off and got swept somewhere. We've got to jump in after it." Lars said with nod.

"Whoa, wait a minute here, Lars. We don't know where this stream will take us. It looks like it's going pretty fast too." Grerr said as he jumped up to his feet and approached the edge.

"I'm telling you guys, let's jump in. I'll bet you anything it'll take us to the monster." Lars grinned as he took a few steps back from the edge.

Lars ran forward and leaped off the edge. A loud splash broke the monotonous sound of the stream as he entered the water. Grerr shook his head and jumped in after him. Izlude muttered to himself about being insane and quickly followed. Soon, the three of them were travelling down the stream at a fairly decent speed, their velocity suddenly increasing faster and faster. It was apparent that something wasn't quite right.

"Hey...bro? Are we supposed to be going this fast? I mean this is starting to get a little freaky." Izlude nervously asked.

"Yeah, I've noticed we've been increasing our speed by quite a lot now, not to mention how loud that roar is." Grerr muttered to no one in particular. "You don't think...? No, it couldn't be!"

Lars and the others saw the waterfall but by then it was too late. Lars muttered some profanities under his breath as he struggled to swim in the opposite direction but the broadsword and flashlight in his hands did not help. The trio were rapidly thrown over the edge of a sixty-foot waterfall. Fortunately their fall was only seven feet. A hidden platform beneath the water's cascade abruptly stopped their fall. Lars stood up and rubbed his knees.

"See? I told you!" Lars laughed, seeing the trail of blood pick up again.

"Yeah...but what would have happened if we kept on going?" Grerr said as he peered over the edge of the platform.

"Never mind about that, we've almost caught up to this monster, I can feel it!" Lars shouted as he charged deeper inside the waterfall cave with his broadsword in his hand.

"Y'know, Izlude, he's running after a seven foot tall creature with large muscles and claws, carrying a weapon that doesn't even use laser technology and a flashlight." Grerr said as he shook his head and the two ran after him.

Grerr and Izlude ran past the various stalagmites on the ground and quickly caught up to Lars, who was standing with his blade ready to strike at the monster's quivering shadow. Lars glanced behind him and shook his head, silencing the two. The monster roared its terrifying roar that shook the pebbles on the ground. A sudden crack sounded from the roof caused the four of them to glance up as a large part of it crashed to the ground, letting in a decent amount of light. The monster looked severely burned and angry at Lars for causing it pain. It limped towards him with its claws extended.

"Get back, guys! It means business!" Lars shouted as he quickly leaped to the left to dodge a swipe that seemed to take great effort.

Lars parried another strike and countered with a slash of his own, clipping off some of what was left of the monster's fur. In fury the monster delivered a hard blow to Lars' torso sending him crashing against the cave wall a good ten feet behind him.

"Damn, you're strong..." Lars groaned, picking himself up and wiping some blood off his lips.

The monster charged forwards, attempting to impale Lars with its claws. Lars, seeing this, dove to the side just in time. The monster, unable to react quick enough, buried its claws deep into the cave wall where Lars had been only moments before. Lars, seeing his opponent struggling against the wall, brought his arms behind his head to stab the creature in the back. The monster pulled one of its claws free and made a swipe for him before he could do anything more than pose as an executioner.

"Whoa!" Lars shouted as his face was almost mauled with only a few inches to spare.

Within moments, the creature was free and marching towards Lars again. He sidestepped another swing but the monster was prepared, sending another blow right after in the direction Lars had dodged. The blow connected, sending him sprawling to the ground and his broadsword off in another direction. Lars glanced at the cat-like behemoth quickly approaching to finish him off.

"Damn it!" Lars cursed as he realized he wouldn't be able to move in time.

A sudden battle cry came from behind the monster and Lars saw the tip of the broadsword protruding from its stomach. Lars tilted his head in a confused state as he watched the creature stumble to the side. It stumbled forwards for a few short meters before reaching the entrance to another area. The monster turned around and roared before collapsing onto the cold floor. The image of Izlude, standing directly behind where it had been, panting heavily, explained everything to Lars.

"Hey, thanks Izlude! I knew there was a reason I took you along!" Lars grinned as he spat up some blood and stood up.

"I-I thought you were going to..." Izlude quietly muttered.

"Hah! You worry too much, Izlude." Lars laughed as he ruffled Izlude's hair.

"That's strange..." Grerr's voice came from the direction of the monster.

Lars turned in its direction and saw Grerr tapping the creature with his foot. Grerr shook his head and brought his hand to his chin, obviously in deep thought. Lars walked up to the creature and examined it more closely.

"It died with its eyes open and its face growling like

that...?" Izlude asked Grerr.

"That's what's so strange. It's like...it was trying to protect something behind this entrance. It didn't want us to go past here." Grerr responded quietly.

"Well," Lars grunted as he pulled the broadsword out of the monster's torso, "let's move it and find out what's behind it."

The trio grunted as they attempted to push, pull, and drag the hulking body away from the path. After several moments of wishing that Kilik had been there to help, they had managed to clear a path. A sudden stench came from behind where it had been.

"Oh, nasty!" Lars coughed as he brought his free hand to cover his mouth and nose.

"Smells like death..." Grerr muttered.

"That makes me feel so much better, Grerr." Lars said with a shake of his head as he plunged inside. "Whoa! Check it out guys, it's safe."

Grerr and Izlude shrugged and entered as well. Before them, they saw several bodies thrown about what appeared to be a nest of some sort. The bodies appeared to be untouched by anything other than time.

"Hey, I think that's Mrs. Crunthammer!" Lars exclaimed, poking her corpse with his broadsword. "I never even noticed she was missing."

"The monster had cubs..." Izlude spoke, his voice slightly muffled by his hand.

Lars turned his head towards Izlude and saw the bodies of three smaller versions of the monster they had just slain. They lay motionless. Two sprawled on their stomachs, one on its back. Their fur appeared to have fallen off completely. They were naked.

"It was only feeding its offspring, it wasn't killing for sport..." Grerr muttered as he turned his back to the cubs and pinched his eyebrows with one hand.

"But they look like they've been dead for a while. Didn't the mother realize it?" Lars responded as he crouched beside one of them, leaning on his broadsword for support.

"Maybe she did. Maybe she just didn't want to realize it. Maybe she thought if she kept bringing them food and acting as a mother should...they would remain alive to her." Izlude suggested.

Silence filled the room as this idea worked its way into their minds. Lars stood up and ran his hand through his hair. He shook his head and then turned to face his comrades. Izlude looked like he didn't know what to think and Lars suspected that he was blaming himself for killing the monster. He strolled up to Izlude and nodded to him.

"It would have been either it or me. The only thing I'm a little upset about is the fact that we could've let it maul the chief up before killing it. C'mon, let's get out of here, alright?" Lars said with a smile.

"And how do you propose we do that? It's a good fifty-foot drop from the platform to the ground, remember?" Grerr replied as he walked out of the decay-filled room.

CHAPTER 3

The water roared constantly as Lars, Izlude, and Grerr stared blankly at the chasm below the platform that had saved their lives earlier. It was apparent that to continue by jumping would not be something they would survive easily.

"There's got to be another way. That monster must've had a quicker and safer route to the town." Lars muttered to no one in particular while leaning against the cave wall with his arms folded over his chest.

The trio stood pondering their situation for quite a while. Eventually fed up with standing still, Lars began pacing back and forth, tapping the blunt side of his broadsword against his leg. Izlude's posture turned to a slouch and he soon conceded to his tired state. He sat down on the ground and rested his head against the cave wall.

"Just like the Mercenaries to easily get into a place and not be able to get out. Really smooth as sandpaper." Grerr muttered to himself.

"We'll get out! Just you wait, Grerr!" Lars shouted as he swung his broadsword abruptly at a nearby stalagmite.

A loud clunk echoed throughout the waterfall cave that sounded like it originated from the room where Lars had fought the monster. Grerr and Izlude froze in place, attempting to listen to any other noises but either the waterfall was too noisy or none else came.

"...the hell?" Lars murmured, slowly approaching the previous room.

As they entered the roofless area, they saw that some contraption had extended from the western wall. It appeared to be some sort of hollow box, one that could easily fit five if there had been that many. The moon's light revealed that the inner walls were metallic chrome.

"You don't see that everyday, eh Izlude? I wonder what it does..." Lars said, tapping the side of it with his broadsword.

"I think...I think maybe we should go inside it." Izlude offered his advice quietly.

Lars turned his head to look at Izlude and shrugged. The three cautiously stepped inside the box and no sooner had Grerr's foot cleared the opening the box closed itself, trapping them inside. Lars quickly approached the side where they had entered just moments before and began to pound his fists against it.

"Out of the frying pan, only to get into the fire. It was a trap." Grerr stated, glaring at Izlude.

"Well, what else were we going to do? Magically go back to the bar-"

Lars was cut off as the box shot upwards. He was thrown backwards and Izlude groaned as Lars landed on top of him. With Lars landing on him, Izlude fell backwards and swept Grerr's feet out from under him. The final result was all three of them on the floor of the box. No sooner had the rapid ascension occurred, it suddenly stopped. The side from where they had entered opened up revealing the bar counter in front of them. It appeared they had come through the floor via another secret passageway. Lars stood up and helped Izlude get back on his feet and then stepped out of the box, leaving Grerr to help himself up.

"I'm not quite sure how that worked, but I like it." Lars said with a grin as he nodded.

Some muffled voices outside made them freeze in their places. Izlude squinted his eyes attempting to see more than shadows out a nearby window but failed terribly. Lars put one of his fingers on his lips trying to hear the conversation.

"...and that's when I decided to wake you from your sleep, Honorable Chief of Drom. I think something horrible has befallen the pub." one of the voices seemed to be saying.

"Uh, oh...It's the chief!" Grerr whispered harshly.

"Damn it! C'mon! Let's get back in that box and see if we can still jump off the waterfall platform!" Lars replied.

"Bro...that'd kill us." Izlude reminded him.

"It'll be less painful than the chief!" Lars growled as he started to make his way back to the contraption.

"Lars!!" the chief's booming voice roared throughout the entire pub.

Lars flinched and slowly turned around to see the village chief, standing tall and muscular. He doubted that the chief could have fit in the doorway walking straight. The chief's signature beard hid most of his face, and his short-cut blonde hair struck a position of power. Lars smiled insincerely at the chief and bowed low.

"To what do we owe the honor of your appearance, Honorable Chief?" Lars sarcastically muttered with a low bow.

"Bro...take it easy, remember how scary he is." Izlude nervously whispered in his brother's ear.

"I should have known it was you and your gang of miscreants!" the chief roared.

"It's not what it looks like! Really, sir!" Grerr replied.

"That's not gonna work, Grerr, it *is* what it looks like." Lars replied shaking his head. "Chief, at first we came in here to steal some alcohol, I'm not gonna lie."

"Aha! I knew it! This time you'll pay for your damages! Guards!" the chief roared.

"Whoa! I said 'at first'!! But then, we saw this light, which lead us to a passageway, which then led us to Jarvis-" Lars began to explain.

"Yes, Jarvis. I'd like to have a word with him for how much you're going to owe him for all this chaos you've caused here!" interrupted the chief.

"Kinda hard to talk to a corpse..." Grerr muttered.

"Oh, the chief will find a way. Goddess knows he yells loud enough." Lars replied quietly.

"Dead?! It wasn't bad enough that you looted his pub, you went and murdered him?!" the chief angrily growled, rage filling his eyes.

"We didn't kill him! Some monster did! The same one who was responsible for everyone in the town getting picked off like flies!" Lars quickly responded.

"You expect me to believe that some monster, hidden beneath a pub of all places is responsible for eight missing people?" the chief snapped as he looked around for the guards he had called a fair while ago.

"*Was* responsible. We slayed it, sir." Grerr replied.

"Oh don't give me that! You guys slaying a monster? Hah! You wouldn't know how to chop wood!" The chief began to laugh at the ridiculous excuse being thrown before him.

The two guards walked in just then, dressed in some crude armor and helmets that looked rustier than Mr. Crunthammer's fishing bucket. Attached to their sides were swords similar to that of Lars' but lacking the shiny luster of his blade.

"Hey Harmon...Marson." Lars greeted them casually with a nod each.

Lars and Izlude had grown up with the twins and used to be very close friends; however, one day several years ago they had entered into an argument, which shattered the friendship. Now they considered each other no more than acquaintances. Lars sighed and turned to face Izlude and Grerr.

"Well, the 'brute squad's here. You just had to open up your mouth, huh Grerr?" Lars said with his hand on his hip.

"Chief, at least let us show you the body! Even you will admit that it couldn't have possibly been us." Grerr pleaded, ignoring Lars' comment.

"You will both be confined in the village jail for a week without food, without sunlight. There you will think hard about the crimes you've committed, and once you have been released you will devote the rest of your lives for the betterment of this village!" the chief growled ferociously.

"Betterment of the village? So you want us to kick you outside and lock the gates?" Lars replied with a grin.

"You, Lars, shall remain in that hole for two weeks without food or sunlight! If that doesn't break that false bravado of yours, I'll eat my hat! Guards, seize them." the chief commanded.

Lars withdrew his broadsword from his belt, spun it around with a flick of his wrist, and brandished it at the approaching guards. Grerr nodded to Lars, smashed a nearby bottle against the bar and held it like a dagger. Izlude backed up slightly behind them, muttering that no good would come of this. He grasped around behind himself for something and managed to get a hold of a fire poker. Harmon paused for a moment, looked in Marson's fearful blue eyes, and then glanced to the chief.

"Uh, sir?...We're outnumbered here." Harmon stated nervously.

"How did we get stuck with such a blockhead for a chief, just listen to us for once. We'll take you to Jarvis' body, alright? You can see that we had nothing to do with it and it'll prove we're innocent. Otherwise, we'll put down our weapons and go quietly. Sound like a deal?" Lars haggled.

The chief clenched his fist in rage, causing his large, muscular arm to quake. Izlude was sure that he would ignore Lars' broadsword at any moment and charge to punch him. After a few stressful moments, the chief unclenched his fist and shook his head.

"As a favor to Daron Nokuten, Lars, I'll allow it. But if you try and run, I will personally see to it that you will regret it for the rest of your life." the chief cautioned.

"Good ol' dad..." Lars Nokuten muttered as he nodded and slinked against the wall towards the library with his broadsword pointed at the twins.

Lars waited for Grerr, Izlude and the others to arrive next to the bookcase. He gestured with his free hand for Izlude to pull back the multi-colored book. Izlude nodded slowly and made his way to beside his brother. He wrapped his fingers around the spine of the book and pulled it out of the bookcase once again. Minutes passed by as the tension began to rise in the library. The bookcase wasn't sliding.

"It figures it was all a lie!" the chief laughed to himself as he realized he had something he could finally pin on Lars.

"Hold on! If it worked once, it'll work twice. Geez, you're so impatient, geezer." Lars sighed.

"If it worked at all!!" the chief growled.

The chief lunged forwards and pulled Grerr towards him. Grerr, being caught off-guard let his broken bottle fall to the ground with a shatter. He struggled to get out of the chief's grip but to no avail, Grerr was easily over-powered.

21

"Drop your sword, Lars! I could break Grerr's neck like a toothpick!" the chief boasted.

"Damn it, Grerr!" Lars cursed through clenched teeth, hesitatingly dropping his broadsword to the cold floor.

Harmon and Marson rushed towards Izlude and Lars. Izlude brought up the fire poker still in his hands but his arms quaked as he brandished it. He was thankful for receiving Lars' headshake, telling him not to fight back. He nodded back and let the metal fall to the ground beside the broadsword. Two skinny guards soon grabbed Lars. Harmon held Lars' forearms behind his back, while Marson pinned Lars upper arms against his body.

"Heh, if the two of you are holding onto me, and the chief's got Grerr...what're you gonna do about Izlude?" Lars chuckled.

Izlude froze in his place. He wasn't sure if Lars was telling him to actually run for it, or if he was just getting in another jab at the chief's incompetence. Harmon and Marson both looked at the chief for guidance and the six of them held an awkward silence for several moments. The chief finally made his move. He easily dragged Grerr behind him as he walked behind Lars. The chief brought up one of his meaty fists and slammed it on top of Lars' head, knocking him unconscious.

CHAPTER 4

"Damn, that hurt." Lars groaned, his eyes adjusting to the darkness of the village prison.

He saw the familiar bodies of Grerr and Izlude in the stone cell they had been placed in. Lars struggled onto his feet and eventually stood like a drunk does, swaying back and forth as if someone invisible kept pulling him different ways. A sharp pain shot into his skull, causing his hand to hold his forehead. Lars shook the pain away and staggered towards Izlude.

"Hey, bro...are you okay? You've been out for hours." Izlude acknowledged him from his seated position with his back against the stone wall.

"Yeah, never been better. I suppose that's gratitude for you. We kill a monster murdering tons of people, and get labelled murderers in the process." Lars sighed.

Grerr was sprawled on what must have been the bed, but in reality was nothing more than a sheet draped over the floor. His arms were behind his head and he was looking at the roof. Izlude noticed Lars glancing at him and shook his head.

"Best not to disturb him, bro...he's not really happy right now." Izlude warned.

"Not happy, huh? Well, he'd better cheer up!" Lars purposely said so that Grerr would hear.

"Cheer up? Cheer up?! You've landed us in the village prison, Lars." Grerr countered.

"Actually, if we want to get specific, it was the chief who landed us here." Lars laughed to himself as he leaned against the wall where Izlude was and slid down to sit on the floor.

Grerr sighed loudly and turned on his side, shunning Lars with his back. Lars made a mocking scowl at Grerr and rested his head against the stone wall. He poked Izlude's head out of boredom, causing Izlude to stare at Lars in confusion.

"Hey, bro...what would our mom think of us if she was alive and saw this?" Izlude broke the silence.

"Your mom? She'd be proud as heck! You're finally

23

starting to follow in her footsteps." Lars responded, taken aback at first.

"...Starting to follow?" Izlude questioned.

"Yeah. In order to follow her fully, you've got to help me figure out a way to get out of here easily. She was always a good escape artist." Lars replied, closing his eyes.

"Escape artist?" Izlude asked as he ignored Lars' sudden disinterest in the subject.

Lars didn't reply. Izlude wasn't sure if he had just fallen asleep or was too preoccupied with their situation to want to bother to talk to him more at the moment. Izlude turned his head away from his brother and stared through the iron bars into the room past it. There were no windows and their only source of light came through a small crack in the roof on the other side. He could see Lars' broadsword leaning there against the far wall with its hilt towards the ceiling. He sighed inaudibly and closed his eyes until the warmth of sleep overcame him. When he opened his eyes next, he found himself alone in a bright room. It had no walls, no ceiling, no air brushing his face and Izlude felt a rush of panic.

"...Izlude..." a youthful female voice spoke out to him.

"Who's there?" Izlude cried out, looking around for its source.

"You don't need to be afraid, Izlude...you're safe here." she replied back with a hint of a giggle.

"...Safe here? Just where is here?" Izlude questioned, kicking the front of his shoes against the bright floor.

"Does that really matter, dear?" the voice giggled again.

"What's going on? Please tell me!"

"Very well. You're about to go on a journey, Izlude," she said, suddenly becoming serious.

"...A journey?" Izlude asked, curiosity getting the better of him.

"Yes, and throughout it you're going to experience much. Just remember to keep your friends close and your enemies closer, and you'll make it just fine." she laughed to herself.

"...E-Enemies?"

"It's time for you to leave this small village where you've

spent the past fifteen years of your life. There will be trying times ahead of you, but I promise that everything is going to be all right. Lars will serve you well. He may not be as predictable as someone in your situation would hope but he'll always be there for you. I'll be watching you, Izlude. It's time for me to say goodbye for now." the voice trailed away.

"W-wait! Don't go! I've got questions! Who are you? Will we meet again?" Izlude frantically shouted in the bright room as it began to fade away.

"I'm simply a friend, and we'll meet again in the near future, I promise..." the voice softly replied.

Izlude was woken up by a strange humming noise coming from around the iron bars. He raised his head and glanced over at Lars. Lars was staring at a trapdoor on the ceiling beyond the iron bars and humming a solitary note with extreme concentration. Grerr was glancing at Lars every now and then and was shaking his head in embarrassment. Izlude stood up and approached Grerr, without taking his eyes off of Lars.

"Uh, bro? What're you doing?" Izlude said as he sat down beside Grerr.

"Shh! I'm getting us out of here!" Lars snapped back and then continued to hum.

"For the last time, Lars. Humming a single note will not cause the trapdoor to magically unlock itself, fling itself open and lower a ladder for us to get out of here." Grerr sighed loudly.

A loud click echoed through the prison originating from the roof. Lars turned around to face Grerr.

"I told you!" Lars said as he cleared his throat and continued to hum.

"It's probably just someone being annoyed at your humming coming down here to beat you up." Grerr replied, flopping backwards with his arms behind his head.

Loud bickering came from the trapdoor. The three were unable to determine what was being said, but they knew that there were two different voices. Finally, the trapdoor swung open and a familiar face stuck their head inside the prison.

"Hey you guys! It's us, Nak and Kilik! We're gonna get you out of there!" Nak shouted happily.

"Boy, did you miss a great party." Lars shouted back.

"If it involved that monster, then no thanks. That's not my idea of a party." Kilik muttered back as he shoved Nak, causing him to fall through the trapdoor. Nak yelled for a few seconds until he crashed onto the hard floor of the prison.

"Damn it, Kilik! Are you trying to kill me or something?!" Nak roared back angrily.

"Yeah. Why?" Kilik replied calmly.

Nak grumbled some profanities and picked himself up off the ground. He looked around the room, squinting his eyes to see past the darkness until eventually finding what he was looking for. Nak clapped his hands together excitedly and grasped onto the ring of keys on the wall. He nodded to them and approached the cell door where Lars, Izlude, and Grerr were waiting.

"No, not that one..." Nak muttered to himself as he began trying random keys.

"Will you hurry it up? It's going to be light out soon!" Kilik shouted into the darkness through the trapdoor.

Kilik shook his head and fumbled with the rope ladder that was tied to a nearby boulder. He examined it slightly and sighed as he thought of all the consequences of his current actions. He eventually shrugged and tossed the ladder down, taking careful aim to hit Nak on the head with the bottom of it.

"Kilik, if you do one more thing to me today, I swear I'll burn your house down." Nak yelled back, rubbing his head.

"I wouldn't be threatening your only way of escaping this place, Nak. You see, I'm the only one up here, and all I have to do is untie this ladder from the boulder here..." Kilik let his voice trail off.

Lars sat on the ground of the cell and leaned forward with his fist against his cheek. He stared at Nak who was still fumbling with the ring of keys and tried his best to ignore Nak's constant mutterings of apology and frustration. He cast his gaze upon Izlude who seemed to be lost in his own little world.

Izlude was indeed deep in thought. He couldn't seem to forget the strange dream he'd had. The words that were said to him sounded so clear. Izlude wasn't sure if he wanted to go on this journey that the mysterious woman in his dreams had spoken about. The thought of leaving the Village of Drom filled his mind with fear. Even though he and Lars were treated as outsiders, Izlude still loved the small, secluded village. Eventually he sighed to himself as he realized that it was probably a dream his mind had concocted after the events earlier that night. Izlude's train of thought was derailed as Lars kneeled behind him and rested his arms on top of Izlude's head.

"What could you possibly be thinking so hard about?" Lars chuckled.

"...Nothing, bro." Izlude muttered, slightly distracted.

"I know! It's girl trouble, isn't it?" Lars replied with a grin.

"Have you ever wanted to leave this village?" Izlude said as he brushed Lars' arms off him and looked him in the eyes.

"Is that a rhetorical question, Izlude? I told you before this is a boring life. The first chance we get, we're leaving this dump as a group. We'll take Grerr, Kilik, and I suppose Nak if he doesn't do something stupid." Lars said, standing up with his hands on his hips.

"So we'll be leaving Nak behind then?" Kilik jabbed.

"Forget it, Lars. I'm not leaving with you. After tonight, I don't think I could take any more of your kind of adventures. In fact, I'm going to stay in this cell here until the chief lets me out." Grerr muttered.

"So you're going to be the chief's slave? What the hell happened to the Grerr I used to know?!" Lars roared, pointing his finger at Grerr.

"I'm sorry, Lars, but maybe the chief's right. Maybe it's time we grew up. You're twenty-one for Goddess' sake, you're not a kid anymore. None of us are..." Grerr muttered as he pretended to go to sleep.

"Well, fine! Kilik'll come. Won't you, Kilik?" Lars sighed, giving up on Grerr and shouting towards the trapdoor.

27

"Hah! Good luck with that. You'd have better odds getting Nak to fool someone into thinking he's normal." came his muffled response.

"Why you backstabbing, lazy bastards. You want to live as farmers the rest of your lives, go ahead. That's not for me, no way. I want to see the world out there, not be stuck seeing this bland scenery every day for the rest of my life! ...Guess it's just Nak and Izlude coming with me then." Lars sighed to himself.

"Maybe Kilik and Grerr are right. I mean we've got it good here..." Nak mumbled sheepishly as he finally unlocked the cell door.

Lars and Izlude left the cell and Lars turned around to face Grerr. He shook his head with a grin.

"Alright, maybe you guys want to live here and be bored, all the power to you. You'll realize sooner or later that you missed out on your chance of a lifetime. I'm leaving tonight along with whoever is coming with me!" Lars shouted, attempting to stare past the roof.

"B-Bro?! Tonight?!" Izlude stammered.

"Yeah, we're out of this joint, Izlude. We'll leave this town to Kilik, Grerr, and Nak." Lars quickly replied as he picked up his broadsword and slid it under his belt once more.

"How the heck are you going to leave town? The gate is locked and guarded." Grerr mumbled from the cell.

"The sky ship that picks up our produce should be here within the hour, and I'm gonna be on it one way or another." Lars laughed.

CHAPTER 5

"Are you insane?!" Nak bellowed into Lars' ear.

Lars winced and put his finger to his lips. He shook his head and brought his attention back to the sky ship in front of him. It towered over everything around it, easily three times the size of the tallest tree in the forest around Drom. Towards the back of the sky ship were two giant propellers lazily turning in the wind and Lars could barely see the flames beneath the sky ship allowing it to hover slightly above the ground. Three armed sailors with machine beam-guns strung over their shoulders were lazily guarding the entrance to the interior of the ship on the starboard side. They were all dressed in their navy-blue uniforms and black combat boots, along with helmets with visors that covered all of their faces but their mouths. One of the sailors leaned against the side of the sky ship and tucked his chin towards his chest. Lars, Nak, Kilik, and Izlude were just close enough to barely hear their conversation.

"Why are we stuck on guard duty again?" replied the middle sailor as he violently smacked the side of his firearm.

"'Cause you had to be 'n idiot 'n get Julius drunk. If it wasn't fer you, he'd be guardin' the ship like he always does!" snapped the one to his left.

"I'm the bartender for Goddess' sake, Jahard! That's my job, getting people drunk! Not holding onto machine beam-guns and freezing my limbs off!" shouted the bartender.

"Will both of you shut it? You're giving me a headache." growled the one leaning against the side of the sky ship.

"This is all Captain Cyrus' fault. The people in this area are country bumpkins. The worst they'd have is a pitchfork. This is stupid! We don't need three people to cover Julius' shift." sighed the middle sailor again.

"Have ye been seein' the size of Julius, Hikari?" replied Jahard.

"Good point. Where the hell are Clark and Orion?" Hikari the bartender complained as he turned to face the last

29

unnamed sailor.

"How the hell should I know? Probably goofing off again. All they gotta do is go to the pick-up point, grab the vegetables, and bring them back. The passengers aren't gonna be too happy with this delay." he said.

"Yer prolly right. They be lazy dogs, those two. Can we tie 'em up and toss 'em off the side o' the Sky Princess later, Tenji?" Jahard grinned, showing some missing teeth.

"No." replied Tenji gruffly, folding his arms over his chest as he rested against the side of the sky ship.

Lars grinned to himself as a plan began to be created in his mind. He turned to Izlude wearing the same grin on his slightly dirty face. Izlude began to stumble backwards.

"B-Bro? W-what're you thinking?" he replied in a harsh whisper as he tripped over a branch behind him and landed on his rear end.

"I'm thinking...that we're going to just walk onto that ship." Lars chuckled as he began pushing his way through the bushes, heading towards the east.

"Lars, they have guns, and you two don't have tickets." Nak hurriedly replied.

"We could always offer Nak to them as a slave in return for two tickets." Kilik suggested.

"Shh, I've got a better plan. Didn't they just mention something about two sailors picking up the shipment taking too long?" Lars began to explain.

"Yeah...what about it?" Izlude coughed as he brushed off his pants.

"The village chief keeps the landing zone and the pickup area far away from the eyes of the villagers, right? He thinks that the less technology we see, the better. The way I see it...we go check out that pickup area, and then..." Lars trailed off as he lowered his head slightly and grinned evilly.

"Knock 'em unconscious and steal their clothes?" Kilik chuckled as he realized Lars' plan.

Lars nodded and Kilik immediately clapped Lars on the back. Kilik nodded in return with a similar grin on his face, and the two immediately began to sprint into the thick underbrush. Nak shrugged and turned to face Izlude.

"Y'know, I think I'm gonna miss Lars when you two go." he sighed, sitting down on the grass beneath him.

"I'm not sure I want to go...he kind of just declared I was going with him." Izlude replied softly.

"Well, he *is* your older brother after all. I mean, I might not be as smart as Grerr, but I know I wouldn't want to live in this village without any family. Heck, if it wasn't for my older sister, I'd go with you guys in a heartbeat, but...she needs me, y'know?"

"Yeah...but there are so many unknowns out there, and it's kind of scary, Nak..." Izlude responded, glancing up at the thousands of stars surrounding the night sky.

"I'll tell you what. If by some miracle you manage to get out of this village, and then you get bored or something horrible happens, my door will always be open." Nak smiled as he patted Izlude on the back.

"Yeah, alright. Thanks." Izlude replied, distracted.

The warehouse walls were filled with cracks and Orion stared at them from his relaxed, seated position. He lazily grabbed another apple from the pile of vegetables beside him and bit into it. Both Clark and Orion knew that their captain, Cyrus, wouldn't miss a dozen or so vegetables. The village supplied a great amount of produce for their sky ship to sell. So they could easily justify why it took them so long to load it all into their cargo hovercraft and deposit it inside the loading dock. Orion took another loud bite into the apple and turned his head slightly to look at Clark who was sitting with his arms folded over his chest and his eyes closed.

"Oy, Clark!" Orion shouted, attempting to wake him.

"Mmhmm?" Clark lazily replied to his partner.

"How long have we been gone from the ship?" Orion questioned as he shifted and lay down on the ground using his elbow to prop himself up.

"Not nearly long enough." came his grumbled response.

"I hear you man, I hear you...what was that?" Orion's response was cut short as a loud crash echoed throughout the warehouse.

Orion was a little ticked off when he saw that Clark looked like he could care less, but he shrugged and got up to investigate. After wandering several dozens of meters away from Clark, Orion noticed just how dark it was inside the warehouse. He fumbled for his flashlight and quickly brought it out.

"Must be my imagination playing tricks on me..." he shrugged to himself.

Orion shook his head and turned around to head back to Clark when he heard a loud clunk and felt a burning sensation radiate from his head. Dazed, he shined his flashlight directly in front of him. There he saw a younger man, with surprisingly bright red hair grinning at him. His green eyes looked like those of a child easily getting away with something. Orion, still dazed, couldn't react in time before Lars delivered a second blow to the head with the hilt of his broadsword. Orion fell to his knees and landed on his stomach, unconscious.

"Nice! Alright, one down, one to go." Lars grinned as he did a couple of quick squats to psych himself up.

"Y'know, I've always wanted to undress someone, but usually it was the other gender. Oh Goddess, it's clammy!" Kilik groaned with disgust as he began to peel off the sailor's uniform.

"You have fun now! I'll go get the second one." Lars laughed.

Clark lazily glanced at his watch, and then swung his head to look in the direction Orion had gone. He couldn't figure out why Orion had suddenly gotten uptight over what Clark thought was probably some giant rat. He had heard rumours in Port Tasuna that there were a lot of unusually sized animals roaming the rural areas of the world. Clark thought he had heard another commotion as well, but decided to shake it from his mind. His sleep was more important to him. Captain Cyrus, after all, demanded a lot of hard work. Clark snapped his eyes open as he felt the sting of a sharp stone that had been whipped at his head.

"Orion, you childish bastard. Enough games! We've only got a few minutes of rest we can milk out of this." Clark called out, getting up.

"Childish bastard? Well that's not very nice." a playful voice replied quickly followed by another stone.

Lars charged forward with his broadsword drawn, hoping to catch Clark off-guard long enough for him to knock the sailor unconscious. The youth from Drom didn't think that Clark was armed and unfortunately Lars was the one caught off-guard. Clark had quickly pulled out his beam saber and ignited it, sending sparks a foot away from their source. It caused an eerie yellow-green glow to fill the room. The only metallic part of Clark's beam saber was the hilt. The rest of the beam saber was the same shape as Lars' broadsword, yet seemed to fluctuate in a laser-like pattern. Lars stopped in mid-stride and planted his feet. He looked at Clark's beam saber wide-eyed and then down at his old-fashioned metallic blade.

"Heh, back down while you still can! You're from Drom, ain't ya? There's no way in hell that that hunk of steel is going to last against technology like this." Clark laughed, slowly marching towards Lars.

Lars' eyes returned to their normal state and a grin slowly began to emerge from lips. He brought his broadsword up and thrust his arm out, pointing the tip a few feet from Clark's head. Clark stared at Lars, taken aback.

"Heh, that's just the thing. I don't think things through!!" Lars roared taking a few quick steps forward and swinging his shiny, metallic broadsword at Clark.

Clark quickly brought up his beam saber, regaining his composure just in time. He laughed to himself as he saw his beam saber slice through Lars' broadsword like butter in his mind's eye. Reality seemed to stun Clark as he saw that his beam saber had no effect on Lars' broadsword. He stared in shock, alternating between Lars' weapon and at Lars himself, who seemed to be equally shocked. Clark felt himself having to struggle against the pressure on his beam saber that was coming from Lars.

"It can't be...I'm using an Arcanian technological weapon! Nothing can withstand a beam saber other than another beam saber! Nothing!!" Clark growled as he forced his muscles to repel Lars' force.

"Well, you've found something else that can withstand it apparently!" Lars smirked, watching Kilik crash a wooden plank on top of Clark's head, knocking him unconscious.

Clark's beam saber fell to the ground with a crackle and the "blade" eventually dissipated until only the hilt remained. Kilik looked down at the crumpled heap that was Clark's unconscious body and grimaced.

"He's gonna have one hell of a headache when he wakes up." Kilik muttered with a sniffle as he tossed Orion's uniform, boots and helmet to Lars.

Lars chuckled as he struggled putting the navy-blue uniform on top of his clothes. He took a glance at the combat boots and checked the size.

"Won't fit me. I'll just have to take a chance and hope they don't look at my feet. As for this helmet..." Lars paused as he sniffed it, "ugh, the things I'll do to get out of here. This stinks of sweat!"

He shuddered and placed it on top of his head. The room immediately turned a greenish hue and Lars was able to see things a lot clearer. After a few short moments of adapting to his night-vision, Lars remembered the clash between his broadsword and the beam saber. He knew that Clark was right. Logically his broadsword should have been melted. Lars shrugged to himself. He was never one to think about things. A quick glance at his broadsword caused him to inspect it closer. The lettering had changed. Whereas before it used to read, " This sword belongs to Jarvis Ghal," it now read, "This sword belongs to Lars Nokuten".

"Weird..." Lars whispered to himself as he poked the lettering.

34

Lars tilted his head, slightly confused, and swung his broadsword a few times in the air. He blinked and slid it into his belt on his left side.

"C'mon, Lars! Help me load the vegetables onto their vehicle. I'm not sure how to use it, but they'll be suspicious if you and Izlude try and board the ship without the produce." Kilik grunted.

"Izlude? Damn it. I just realized. He's still a kid. There's no way he'd fit into one of these uniforms." Lars slapped his forehead.

"Well, just hide him in the produce and sneak him in. That'll work, right?" Kilik sighed as he dropped a large armful of vegetables onto the hovercraft.

"No, it won't. Two people came out, they're going to expect two people to board." Lars replied.

Lars leaned against the hovercraft and put the side of his index finger over his mouth, lost in thought. Kilik looked like he was struggling to think then his face suddenly lit up and he looked over at Lars.

"Alright, I got it. But you're going to owe me big time." Kilik said.

CHAPTER 6

"Are you sure you know how to drive this thing?!" Kilik shouted as Lars tore through the forest with the hovercraft.

"No, but we haven't hit anything yet either!" Lars shouted in reply.

Kilik and Lars were dressed in Clark and Orion's uniforms, helmets included. They had left the pair in the warehouse with an apology note on the floor in front of them.

"Haven't hit anything?! What about half the forest animal population?!" Kilik shouted, shutting his eyes as the hovercraft fell a good ten feet then continued on its path back to the sky ship.

"Well, it was kinda getting crowded in there anyways." Lars stated with a chuckle as he cranked the steering wheel hard to the left.

A large boulder suddenly appeared in front of the hovercraft. Kilik looked at Lars and vice versa. The two then looked back at the boulder and screamed loudly. Lars, in the middle of his scream, pulled back on the steering wheel, causing the hovercraft to propel itself in the air slightly more. A loud scraping noise came from beneath them but the hovercraft cleared the obstacle.

"Lars." Kilik replied in his normal voice.

"Yes, Kilik?" Lars replied.

"Let's never do that again."

"Agreed."

Izlude and Nak snapped out of their thoughts as a loud roar broke the silence. The two looked at each other in bewilderment.

"Is the sky ship leaving?" Izlude hopefully asked.

If it were then maybe he'd have a chance to convince Lars

not to leave. He knew he'd have better odds at getting picked to be chief than that, but even a small chance was something. The loud crash of a tree hitting the ground caused Nak and Izlude to jump. Nak shook his head, silently disagreeing with Izlude. Nak stood up and tried to peer through the darkness ahead of him. His expression immediately turned to one of panic as he threw himself to the side. Any moment later the hovercraft would have hit Nak.

"Darn it! Turn around and try again! We almost got him!" Kilik jokingly laughed.

Kilik jumped out of the hovercraft and landed gracefully on the ground. He walked around and took a low bow in front of Izlude and Nak. Nak spat out a few leaves and glared at Lars who was sitting at the steering wheel. Lars climbed out of the driver's seat and approached Izlude.

"Alright, here's the plan. Kilik is going to help us get into the sky ship. He'll play the role of Clark-" Lars began.

"Orion. Clark's as smart as a brick." Kilik interjected.

"Fine, he'll be Orion. Izlude, we'll sit up front, while you hide underneath all the vegetables in the back. If all goes well, we'll get on the ship, Kilik will quickly hop off before it leaves and no one's the wiser. Any questions?" Lars said.

"Yeah, uh...where *are* Clark and Orion, Lars?" Nak questioned.

"Right here, moron. We're standing in front of you." Kilik shouted as he slapped Nak's forehead.

"You know what I meant!" Nak complained, rubbing where Kilik had swatted him.

"Sleeping like babies back at the warehouse. Now let's go!" Lars commanded.

The three older members of the Mercenaries began piling all sorts of vegetables and fruits on top of Izlude until not a single shred of him was visible. Satisfied, Lars turned around to face Nak. He stared at him for a few moments before thrusting out his hand and holding it before an astonished Nak. Nak flinched slightly, but then smiled at his leader. He grasped Lars' hand firmly and shook it. Lars nodded in silent thanks and hopped into the driver's seat. Kilik did a quick two-finger salute to Nak and got inside the hovercraft. Lars placed his foot gently on the pedal and the hovercraft slowly began to approach the sky ship.

"Why couldn't you have driven like this in the first place?" Kilik sighed.

When Lars had started to cause the hovercraft to move for the second time, Kilik had tensed his muscles, waiting for an inevitable impact. Now he felt he was able to relax, but he was still annoyed at Lars for the joyride in the forest.

"Well, that's because I just found the brakes right now." Lars replied.

"Just...? You just found the brakes right now?! We were driving without being able to stop?!" Kilik roared.

"Keep quiet, the sailors will hear you. They're just up ahead." Lars whispered harshly.

"Yeah, yeah. Tenji, Jahard, and Hikari, right?" Kilik asked, turning his head to look out his window into the night.

Hikari snapped his body towards the direction of the sudden noise and pointed his machine beam-gun. His hands shook the metallic firearm from nervousness. Jahard shook his head and forced the gun towards the ground with his hand.

"Ye shake more than a ship bein' steered by a drunken cap'n, yer liable to shoot us all!" Jahard reprimanded.

"Yeah, just relax kid. It's the hovercraft, that's all. Orion and Clark are finally done with their vacation it seems." Tenji replied, still leaning against the sky ship.

"Kid? I'm nineteen! Almost as old as you are, Tenji!" Hikari protested.

"But I've got several more years onboard the Sky Princess than you. You're just a kid." Tenji sighed.

"Quit yer yammerin', Hikari! Help me open up the belly fer the grub." Jahard grunted from a few meters away.

Hikari sighed deeply and began to make his way towards Jahard. He just wanted the night to be over. He missed his bar and all of the tips from the guests on board. Hikari didn't mind serving the sailors, but he would much rather serve a guest than a fellow man of the sky. His reasons weren't simply monetary gain. He knew that the guests more than likely had a lot of money on them, which meant more money for him. He also knew that the sailors made the same wages as him, minus tips. That being said, if he made a lot of money off of them and caused them to suddenly become broke he could quite possibly end up with a couple of black eyes the next morning. On the other hand, if he refused to pour them drinks, it could be just as painful.

The hovercraft slowly emerged from the forest into the clearing and Tenji jogged over to the driver's side. He began to walk beside it as it slowly approached the sky ship.

"Took you long enough. We get a good haul?" Tenji questioned.

Lars froze and nervously glanced to his right at Kilik who also seemed to share the same sentiment. Tenji sighed and shook his head, still facing forwards.

"It probably wasn't even worth it as usual." Tenji coughed.

Lars cleared his throat and tried his best to remember how Clark spoke to him. Kilik glared at Lars from under his helmet's visor. He shut his eyes as he realized what Lars was about to do.

"Uh, no, Hikari. Not much." Lars replied in a badly altered voice.

Tenji froze in his steps and the hovercraft pulled ahead of him a few meters. Kilik slapped the back of Lars' head violently.

"Moron! That was Tenji, not Hikari!!" Kilik whispered harshly.

Tenji quickly picked up his machine beam-gun that was slung over his shoulder and sprinted to the hovercraft. He jabbed the butt of his firearm against the side of it.

"Stop the vehicle and get out!" Tenji ordered loudly.

"Sorry, Tenji. Haven't been feeling well lately, and you

39

know how much we all look alike in these uniforms." Lars apologized.

Tenji considered this for a moment and lowered his firearm. He was still a little suspicious, but he knew that both Clark and Orion were oddballs. Tenji was fairly certain they were playing one of their games with him.

"Whatever. I'm sick and tired of staying outside. Just drive the hovercraft into the loading dock and let the automated sorting system deal with it all. I'll go relieve Hikari and Jahard and head to the crew's quarters with them." Tenji saluted lazily and ran ahead of the hovercraft towards the massive sky ship that was growing in size as they approached it.

Kilik and Lars breathed a large sigh of relief as they watched Tenji disappear into the ship along with Jahard and Hikari. Kilik shook his head and motioned with his free hand towards the open entrance into the loading dock.

"After you, my good sir." Kilik said, dripping with sarcasm.

Lars placed his foot on the pedal hard and recklessly sent the hovercraft flying into the underside of the ship. An unknown force halted the hovercraft immediately before Kilik could swat Lars again. The loading dock was filled with various mechanical contraptions that Lars and Kilik could only guess at their purpose. A loud female voice boomed throughout the loading dock.

"Please step out of the hovercraft and keep a minimum of a twenty-foot distance from the automated sorting system while it is in operation." it spoke in a monotonous voice.

"Uh, yes ma'am! You heard her, Izlude! Out you go." Lars replied.

Izlude groaned as he pulled himself out of the mound of vegetables in the back. He stumbled off the hovercraft and leaned against a nearby wall. The room was swimming in front of Izlude, causing him to shut his eyes tightly to avoid getting sick. Kilik looked at Izlude and then back at Lars with a grin covering his face.

"You know, I thought it was bad enough in the passenger seat with you driving, but I forgot about Izlude. He must've gone through worse hell." Kilik chuckled.

Lars laughed along with his fellow Mercenaries' member. The laughter died after a short while, leaving nothing but an awkward silence. Lars took off his helmet and looked at Kilik.

"Are you sure you're not going to come with us?" Lars questioned.

"Yeah, Grerr and Nak would be lost as hell without me. Well, probably just Nak. I'll see you when you get back, alright?" Kilik replied with a wave.

He quickly turned around and walked up the metallic ramp that led to the inside of the sky ship. Kilik's feet barely had enough time to both touch the ground before the ramp began raising itself.

"Hey, you take care of yourself, alright Kilik?" Lars shouted loudly.

"Yeah, yeah. I give you a week tops." came his muffled response.

Lars nodded with a smile. He would miss Kilik and the others but he knew he'd be back to the small Village of Drom. Izlude was nervous as he watched the ground slowly distance itself from the sky ship through the loading dock door. He was leaving his home behind and his meager possessions. A tear slowly began to form and it suddenly dripped down his cheek. He wiped it away with his hand quickly and straightened himself up.

"Where are we going now, bro? What are we going to do?" Izlude asked Lars.

"The heck if I know, but we'll figure something out." Lars replied.

Severely muffled shouting could be heard from far beneath the sky ship. Lars frowned in confusion and glanced outside. Orion and Clark were sprinting towards the sky ship as it was taking off. Both were clad in nothing but their boxers and were waving their arms frantically. Lars jabbed his finger repeatedly against the glass and laughed heartily. Izlude and Lars watched as the two tried to run past Kilik, who had been waving at them as they departed. Kilik quickly grabbed one of each of their arms and swung them forwards. The two sailors collided into each other, knocking themselves unconscious again. Kilik dusted himself off slightly and returned to waving. Lars shook his head with a smile.

"Goodbye, Drom! See you in my nightmares!" Lars shouted happily.

"Do you think we'll be okay?" Izlude asked quietly.

"Yeah, we'll be alright. Word of advice though don't touch anything down here." Lars joked as he began to make his way out of the loading dock, carefully winding his way through machinery.

CHAPTER 7

Lars squirmed relentlessly against the heavy, metal chains that bound him. To his right was Izlude, in the same predicament as he was. They had both stumbled into the passenger lounge level of the Sky Princess, where Lars had discovered a large sofa with an antique table placed in front. He had thrown himself on top of said sofa and propped his feet on the table, letting several clumps of dirt fly loose. Lars then proceeded to order a sandwich, much to Izlude's protest seeing as they didn't have a single credit on them to pay. Lars had dismissed Izlude and ordered it anyways.

While Lars was about to take a bite out of his turkey breast sandwich on rye, several sailors entered to do a routine ticket check. Since neither Lars nor Izlude could produce a ticket and they were severely outnumbered, they had no choice but to surrender. Lars had his broadsword taken from him yet again by who could only be Julius, based on his size, and the two of them were dragged from the passenger lounge. Several rich guests seemed glad and in fact applauded the sailors.

Now surrounding them all on the upper, open deck of the Sky Princess was the entire population of sailors. They were throwing insults and appeared to be quite angry, but both Lars and Izlude were unable to hear a majority of what was being said. The wind blowing about their faces was enough to mute even the loudest of the sailors. A large, robust man grunted as he forced his way through the crowd towards Lars and Izlude, seconds from being thrown off the sky ship several tens of thousands of feet in the air. He scowled at the two stowaways, his thick, white handlebar moustache blowing fiercely in the wind but the wind was nowhere near as fierce as the look in his eyes, which caused even Lars to flinch at one glance.

"These two stowaways may very well bring the lady of the skies to strike us down where we stand! Every one of you knows how much terrible luck this has created for us! So I ask you, gentleman, what should we do with them to satisfy the

43

quench of our curse?" Captain Cyrus roared to the angry mob of sailors.

Several shouts of, "Throw 'em overboard!" blasted through the wind towards the two helpless youths.

"N-Now wait just a darn minute! Can't I suggest something?" Lars stammered.

"Very well, what do you propose we do?" Captain Cyrus growled.

"Well, I'm kinda hungry." Lars quickly replied.

Captain Cyrus blinked and suddenly burst into a hearty laugh. He wheezed as he tried to catch his breath, pointing at Lars and eventually placing both hands on his knees in a muffled guffaw. Cyrus then stood up and grinned at the chained stowaways from Drom.

"My apologies, but you'll be thrown overboard. It's the only way we'll be sure we won't be cursed." Cyrus uttered through semi-chuckles.

Cyrus raised his foot to kick them off the side of the ship and just as he was about to do so, a voice emerged from the crowd.

"Wait! There might be another way!" the voice yelled.

"Hikari, what do you mean?" the captain replied without taking his gaze off Lars.

"Well, suppose we made them sailors? They wouldn't be stowaways then, right? We could always use a couple extra hands on deck, and when we reach Port Tasuna we can drop them off." Hikari replied.

"Hmm, you may have a point there. Alright then, starting tomorrow, you're fledgling sailors. Now if you'll excuse me, it's extremely late and I have our detour to co-ordinate. Since you're so set on sparing them, Hikari, I'll trust you to show them the ropes. Julius, give the man his sword back." Cyrus commanded.

He then forced his way through the crowd of sailors who appeared to be stunned. After a few short moments, they shrugged and muttered to each other and disappeared beneath the upper deck, leaving only Hikari and Julius. Julius growled and dropped Lars' broadsword on the wooden deck before walking away. Hikari fumbled with his pockets for a moment before pulling out a key. Without Hikari's helmet on, Lars and Izlude could see his icy-blonde hair blowing in the wind.

"You guys owe me a ton, so don't screw up and make me look bad, alright?" Hikari sighed, freeing Lars and Izlude from their chains.

"Thank you, sir." Izlude replied with a bow.

"Sir? Whoa, whoa, whoa. Never call me 'sir,' that's an insult. It's just Hikari, alright?" he chuckled.

"Oy, Hikari! You be seein' Orion or Clark? I haven't seen 'em since they brought tha' shipment from Drom inside." Jahard questioned, jogging up to Hikari.

"Those lazy bums. I swear, they're going to get it some day." Hikari sighed.

"Yeah, about that..." Lars coughed, attempting to hide his smile as he explained the events prior to their boarding of the ship.

Hikari and Jahard glanced at each other and burst into a fit of laughter. Hikari smacked Lars on the back and smiled largely.

"We're going to get along just fine! Man, if you weren't a guy, I'd kiss ya!" Hikari laughed.

"Oy, Lars and Izlude was it? I'll be takin' you down below the ship to the crew's quarters, a'right? The cap'n said yer sailors tomorrow, so git a good night's rest. Ye'll be needin' it." Jahard cautioned as he motioned for them to follow him.

Jahard had led them far below the ship where passengers weren't allowed. If they had, Lars was fairly certain that they would have turned their noses up in disgust. The floor looked like it hadn't been swept in ages and various hammocks littered the room, some occupied, some vacant. Loud snoring could be heard coming from the occupied hammocks causing

Izlude to cover his ears.

"Don' worry. Ye'll git used to it eventually, we all ha' to."
Jahard explained.

Jahard motioned to a dirty mattress on the floor. Several
holes decorated it and a puff of dust flew a few feet into the air
as Lars prodded it with his foot.

"Just cause yer good buddies of ours, ye'll be gettin' the
royal treatment." Jahard grinned, showing a couple of teeth
missing.

"Royal treatment, eh? I'd hate to see peasant treatment."
Lars muttered inaudibly.

"Well, I'll be leavin' ya to yer dreams, a'right?" Jahard
waved, walking back upstairs to the deck above.

Lars sighed and flipped the mattress over, causing a large
wave of dust to assault their feet and ankles. He then yawned
largely and rubbed his belly.

"Man, I'm still hungry, y'know. Oh well, I'm sure we'll get a
big breakfast in the morning. Night, Izlude." Lars sighed,
sprawling out on the left side of the mattress.

"Night, bro..." Izlude replied.

Izlude glanced down at his brother his bright-red hair
already messed up, and sighed. They were only a day out of
Drom and were already in a heap of trouble. Izlude slowly got
on the mattress next to Lars and shut his eyes, trying to block
the noise of the sailors' snoring and that of Lars' who
somehow seemed to be louder than all of them combined.
Izlude pulled his tattered jacket over his ears and after a few
moments managed to fall asleep.

"We meet again, Izlude." the same female voice echoed a
giggle.

Izlude glanced around again. He found himself in the same
white room he had been in the last time he had fallen asleep.

"How do you know my name?" Izlude replied, sitting down
on the white floor.

"I know a lot more about you than you think, but that's not
important now." the voice stated.

"I think it's important!" Izlude yelled in response.

"Always so serious...you have traces of your mom in you,

but it's been hidden by years of being brainwashed in Drom."
the voice sighed.

"My mom? You knew her?" Izlude whispered, slightly
confused.

"Not exactly. But we'll get into that another day, it's time
for you to start your duties." the voice giggled, fading away
again.

Izlude was hastily shaken awake. He sat up and blinked at
Tenji, suited up in his impressive uniform, and nodded. A
loud, sudden snore pierced Izlude's ear causing him to flinch.
Tenji sighed and shook his head as he walked away.

"Get him up. He'll be in the bar helping out Hikari today,
you're to report to the upper deck. It needs to be scrubbed."
he said, looking back slightly and then continuing on his way.

Lars lazily stumbled through the automatic, metallic sliding door into the bar and yawned largely. He scratched his lower back and approached Hikari, who was busy pouring and mixing drinks for the various passengers in the room. Hikari gave Lars a nod.

"Finally up, eh? I was about to give up on you. You were supposed to report to me two hours ago!" he scolded, flipping a bottle behind his back and catching it in front of him.

"Yeah, and I missed breakfast too apparently." Lars grumbled through squinted eyes.

"Heh, I'll get you something to eat during our break. Meanwhile, you're going to be my porter. Basically keep me stocked on glasses and alcohol." Hikari explained.

Izlude collapsed onto his knees and let go of the mop in his hands. He wiped the sweat off his forehead with the back of his hand and looked at his handiwork. Jahard walked over to him and patted him on the back.

"Tha's a good start, bu' yer only a third o' the way done! C'mon, Izlude! Push it! Put some muscles on tha' body o' yours!" Jahard cheered.

Izlude sighed and picked himself up off the ground. He dipped his mop into his bucket of soapy water and dropped it onto the wooden deck. Izlude grunted as he began to convince the heavy, water-soaked mop to move.

"Hey, Jahard?" Izlude asked suddenly.

"Yep?" Jahard answered from his comfortable observation post on top of some nearby crates.

"Why is it wooden up here? I mean, other than the upper deck most of the Sky Princess is metal." Izlude continued his question while focusing on a particularly dirty spot.

"Well, y'see, several hundreds o' years ago back'n there wasn't any ships in th' skies there used t'be ones on th' seas. They used t'be made o' wood, so in order to keepin' things traditional Captain Cyrus decided t'remodal th' upper deck and replace all th' metal with this 'ere wood. If ye be askin' me, he jus' did it fer the passengers. Makes fer some good tourist photos, y'know what I be sayin' kiddo?" Jahard said with a smile.

"I don't think the dishwasher likes me." Lars said, wringing his shirt of several ounces of water.

Hikari blinked at Lars in shock, unsure whether to laugh or sigh in disappointment. He had sent him into the kitchen with the simple task of placing a few glasses in the dishwasher to be washed to prepare for the evening crowd. Hikari's porter now stood in front of him looking quite like a drowned rat. Lars' bright, red hair was flattened against his forehead and a frown of confusion occupied his face.

"You really are a country bumpkin, huh? Guess I should've figured that, I mean, you snuck on from Drom right?" Hikari finally conceded a chuckle, "Well, I guess if the dishwasher is on the fritz, we'd might as well take our breaks now."

Lars ran his fingers through his hair and nodded, looking forward to some food. Hikari flicked a switch and an electronic sign slid up from the bar counter stating that he would be back in ten minutes. They then left the lounge and after a few moments of walking entered the employee break room. Hikari flopped himself down on a tattered couch and spread his arms across the back of it.

"I've got big plans, Lars." Hikari nodded to himself.

"Big plans?" Lars questioned as he sat himself down on a metal chair.

"Yep, as soon as I find myself an Arcanian artifact, I'll sell it to the highest bidder and retire early. You can count on that." the bartender sighed.

"You're not going to find anything being stuck on this sky ship." Lars pointed out.

"I just wish I could be like Marina: free as the wind." Hikari looked away, lost in thought.

"Marina?" Lars questioned, snapping Hikari back to reality.

"The greatest treasure hunter in Port Tasuna. I used to live next to her growing up, at least before she moved with her sister outside of town. Then she went off to hunt for old relics and I became a sailor. We see each other every now and then when she hitches a ride on the Sky Princess after her treasure hunting."

"Port Tasuna?" Lars asked with a curious look upon his face.

"Oh come on! Do you know anything? Port Tasuna's the hotspot for trading, transportation, information, the works. It's our ultimate destination, but Captain Cyrus is taking us on a minor detour, most likely to pick up Marina, if you ask me. He's good friends with her." laughed Hikari.

"Yeah, that port sounds kind of familiar. Feels like I've been there before when I was younger." Lars replied, deep in thought.

"No way. You would've remembered Port Tasuna. Once you've been there, you'll never want to be anywhere else. That port can make you or break you." Hikari chuckled, standing up.

CHAPTER 8

Several days later, Izlude and Lars were on their mattress. Lars was flopped back with his arms behind his head. Izlude was sitting cross-legged beside him. It had been a particularly long day and Izlude grimaced as he squeezed his left bicep. Lars casually glanced at him and chuckled.

"You're building more muscles! Jahard must have you working up a storm." Lars said.

"Jahard keeps telling me that I need more muscles if I want to be a sailor." Izlude softly answered.

"Well yeah, most of the guys on this ship except Hikari are brawny. I mean, take a look at Julius! He's what, six foot four and four hundred pounds? Don't forget that we're only hitching a ride though. We're going to get off at Port Tasuna when it docks." Lars said.

A loud bell began to ring throughout the sailors' quarters. Several sailors sprung out of their hammocks and shouted as they quickly threw their uniforms on.

"Are we under attack?!" Izlude asked Lars hurriedly.

Lars sat up and listened for a few moments with a quizzical look upon his face before shaking his head.

"No explosions...no screams...no sudden falling feeling...nope, not an attack." Lars sighed disappointedly as he fell backwards onto the mattress again.

Hikari approached the bed and prodded Lars with his foot. He was fully clad in his navy-blue sailor's uniform and his helmet reflected Lars face as he looked up at Hikari.

"Get up on deck! Captain Cyrus wants us to all greet Marina officially." Hikari ordered.

"Yeah, yeah, I'll get there in a second." Lars yawned, closing his eyes.

Hikari sighed and began to run up the steps. He paused for a moment before turning to face the two stowaways from Drom.

"She's pretty cute, Lars!" he yelled.

"Right, let's get up on deck, shall we?" Lars snapped

awake.

The moment Lars and Izlude emerged from the depths of the Sky Princess, they were nearly bowled over by a pair of sailors sprinting past them with a large bundle of rope in their hands. If Lars hadn't extended his arm and quickly pulled Izlude out of the way, he certainly would have been run over. Izlude felt overwhelmed as he tried to keep track of what was going on.

"Hey! Watch where you're going!" Lars shouted at their backs.

When no response came, Lars shook his head. Before he could say anything a crew member shouted loudly to overwrite the chaos that was occurring on the upper deck.

"Captain Cyrus' guest is boarding the ship now!" came the sailor's voice.

Lars squinted into the darkness on the starboard side of the ship and saw that they were hovering just beside a large island in the middle of the sky. It seemed to have some sort of self-propulsion that allowed it to remain thousands of feet in the air indefinitely.

"Take a look at that, Izlude. Don't see that every day, huh?" Lars said without removing his eyes from the sight.

Izlude stood on his toes and looked where Lars was staring. He felt mesmerized by the island and found it difficult to look away. Captain Cyrus bellowed and made his way over to the bow of the sky ship along with the entire population of sailors on the upper deck. Cyrus straightened himself up and tilted his hat down before coming to attention. The sailors each grabbed onto one of two thick ropes and began hauling what appeared to be a heavy load. After some moments of pulling, the small docking platform was finally on level with the starboard side of the sky ship. In the middle of the platform, surrounded by wooden treasure chests bound with rope, stood a young woman. She looked no older than Lars and produced a large smile as she did a small leap over the edge of the sky ship. She effortlessly landed in front of the captain and shook her head. Her light green, shoulder length hair seemed to shimmer in the artificial light that was shining in her direction.

"C'mon, Cyrus! You're always so formal with me." she laughed, sticking her tongue out slightly.

"You'll have to forgive me, Marina. It's hard for me to be informal to a lady." he replied as he took his captain's hat off his head and placed it on his chest.

"Is this the same guy that was about to kick us off this sky ship from forty thousand feet in the air?" Lars rolled his eyes and rested his elbow against the railing.

"But it's good to see you! Any luck with the treasure hunting?" he cheerfully asked while glancing at the platform in front of him.

"I was surprised I didn't find anything Arcanian! It was like one trap after the next! Some bumbling adventurer would probably have activated them all, but not me! I thought I was done for when these two boulders came chasing after me. Good thing I found a cave in the side of a wall or I don't know what might've happened!" Marina hurriedly replied as she fidgeted with a leather whip on her hip.

"Now, now. Let's not wreck a good story. Let's head to my quarters and you can tell me all about your latest adventure." Cyrus interrupted, placing a brawny arm over her shoulder.

"Sure!" she replied as she turned to face the crowd of sailors around her, "You guys make sure to take care of my treasure now. Just bring it all down to my quarters for later, alright?"

Marina smiled and winked at them, which caused several of the sailors to boisterously shout out, "Yes ma'am!" and get to work right away. She giggled and let Cyrus guide her to the entrance to the inner areas of the sky ship where Lars and Izlude were standing. Marina cast a glance in their direction and stopped in her tracks. She scratched her head and talked to Cyrus without taking her eyes off them.

"Who are these guys?" she asked as she placed her hand on her chin, analyzing them.

"Oh, just some fledgling sailors we picked up in Drom." he answered with a cough.

"Well, could you introduce us properly, Captain?" Marina smiled.

"Right. I'm sorry. I've forgotten my manners again. In all the chaos that's been going on lately, I don't even know their names myself. We've been shorthanded as is without Clark and Orion going A.W.O.L on me." Cyrus grumbled, fiddling with his handlebar moustache.

"I'm Marina Jayd, and you are?" she extended her hand towards Lars.

"Lars Nokuten, and this is my younger brother, Izlude Nokuten." he answered, shaking her hand casually.

"Well, it's nice to see some new faces on the Sky Princess. Good luck with your ship-work!" she said with a nod and the two of them walked down the stairs towards the inner sanctums of the sky ship.

"Man, Hikari wasn't kidding!" Lars chuckled to himself.

He lazily turned his head from the stern of the ship to face the bow and his gaze met with Julius', his eyes only an inch from Lars' face. His body was nearly bent in half as he leaned forward to accomplish this.

"Whoa!" Lars shouted as he leapt away from the hulk of a man, "Don't scare me like that!"

"Get moving you slime! You need to move this treasure to Marina's quarters! It's the second door on the left when you're on the level directly below this one. And if either of you even thinks about stealing from her, you'll be thrown off the ship! Now move it!" he ordered, following Marina and Cyrus.

"Now wait just a minute! Where the heck are you going, Julius?!" Lars shouted.

"To hear Marina's story! Now get to work!" came his response.

"Well, that's just great. Julius could have carried all of those chests by himself in one trip. At least we've got the other sailors to help." Lars muttered to Izlude.

54

"Uh, bro...? They're down there too..." Izlude replied.

"What?!" Lars shouted and winced as he looked around the now empty deck.

"I don't care if I never see another treasure chest for as long as I live." Lars groaned as he sat on a particularly large one he had just hauled inside Marina's quarters.

The room seemed almost extravagant with royal red curtains, a thick carpet, large bed, and several dressers. Izlude curiously walked into an adjacent room and gasped.

"Lars! She has her own personal shower! Remember how you used to fight with Kilik for first dibs on the waterfall?" Izlude exclaimed.

"Yeah, but where's the fun in that?" Lars sighed, resting his elbows on his knees. "Don't go snooping around too much. I'm just catching my breath for a bit and then we'll go down below and sleep."

The door to Marina's quarters slowly opened and the treasure hunter from Port Tasuna jumped backwards, startled.

"Oh! I didn't know anyone was in here." she said as she entered the room and closed the door behind her. "Lars was it?"

"Yeah, Julius had us bring all of your treasure here. Honestly, if that guy wasn't five times my size, I'd show him a thing or two!" Lars shouted, swinging his broadsword around in the air.

"Oh? Then why don't I go and bring him here so you can do that?" Marina asked.

She placed her hand on the doorknob and pulled the door open slightly with a grin. Marina laughed as Lars made a mad sprint for the door and quickly pushed it shut.

"Uh, that's not necessary at all!" he stammered.

"If you say so." Marina giggled in response.

"So, how much is all this treasure worth?" Lars asked, curiously.

"Treasure? It's junk! Most of it, anyways. I had to say it was worth some value to save face. To be honest, I've studied most of the eras of the ancient past as a hobby and I have yet to find anything worth more than a few hundred credits. I'm afraid treasure hunters like me are a dying breed. Less things to be found each day, you know? I guess that's why Arcanian artifacts are worth so much. Hardly any of them left." Marina said as she sat down on a nearby chair and began to take her leather boots off.

"Um, Marina? Who were the Arcanians?" Izlude quietly questioned from the bathroom doorway.

Marina and Lars stared at him causing him to think he had asked the wrong question. Izlude looked down at the carpet and fiddled with the bottom of his tattered shirt. After a few moments of awkward silence, Marina burst into a hearty laugh.

"I never told you about the Arcanians, Izlude?" Lars asked his brother with a frown, to which Izlude shook his head.

"Allow me, Lars. The Arcanians are anyone who lived during the Arcanian era thousands of years ago. It was a time of peace, prosperity, and technological advances like you never dreamed were possible. Things like magic were commonplace and not completely forgotten like they are today. They were masters of mixing magic with technology and as a result, most of what you see in the modern world is the result of them. Of course, it's not like we know how any of the artifacts work at the start, which is why once certain ones are discovered they're bought by the highest bidder and reverse-engineered." Marina explained.

"If they were so advanced, what happened to them?" Izlude quietly responded.

"That's the thing, people don't really know. There's no records or anything, so it's a great mystery. Of course, there's always the thing of legends which fuels most people's dreams these days." Marina looked up, deep in thought.

"The thing of legends?" Lars raised an eyebrow.

"The Crystal of Immortality." Marina nodded.

"Crystal...of Immortality?" Izlude repeated.

"Now, there's no guarantee this artifact even exists, but it's rumored that an Arcanian grand mage poured his heart and soul into creating an item that has the power to make its owner immortal. The story says that this grand mage's wife had contracted a terrible disease, which didn't have a known cure. After giving up on the doctors and healers, he turned to the essences of all the elements in the world: fire, earth, water, lightning, ice, and wind. After journeying halfway across the world collecting these elements, he returned home and compressed all of them so much that they fused together. That being done, he placed a crystal shell around them for protection in case the unstable fusion ever broke.

The sad thing is, by the time he had done all of this he had contracted the disease as well and was far too weak to unlock its powers. Scared of what others might do to him once they discovered what he had created, the grand mage took the artifact away and with his dying steps hid the Crystal of Immortality in an unknown location. It's rumored his skeleton is still holding onto it to this day."

"Well, that was a great bed time story, Marina, but I'm wasted from hauling down all that junk of yours. I'm off to bed." Lars yawned as he motioned for Izlude to join him.

"Fledgling sailors always have the roughest work. You'd better get some rest because it's a whole new work day tomorrow!" Marina nodded and laughed as she heard Lars' groan from the hallway.

CHAPTER 9

Izlude awoke with a start. He snapped his head to his left and right searching for his brother Lars, but without any success. He blinked and looked around the rest of the room for any sign he hadn't overslept. The various hammocks strung about the room lay still with no one inside them. Izlude panicked as he quickly got to his feet and sprinted to the upper deck where he knew Jahard was waiting to scold him for neglecting his duties on board the sky ship.

"I'm so sorry, Jahard! I must have been...tired...?" Izlude slowed his speech down as he looked around the spotless upper deck.

Izlude eventually brought his gaze up and saw Marina sitting on some crates looking up at the sky. The mop and bucket lay still a few feet below her, reflecting in the freshly washed deck.

"Hey, you'll never be a full-fledged sailor if you can't get up on time! Good morning, Izlude! Looks like a hot one today. At this rate though, you've got a long way to go if you want to be a better sailor." she laughed, patting the crates beside her with her hand.

Izlude nodded and scrambled up on top of the crates. He paused for a moment to catch his breath before looking up at Marina's head. She was only a few inches taller than he was so this wasn't a difficult feat.

"Well, Lars and I...we're not really sailors." Izlude said shyly.

"That's funny. I could have sworn Cyrus said you were new sailors." Marina responded, taken aback.

"It's a little complicated, but...we were caught as stowaways and then Captain Cyrus was going to throw us off the ship because of it being bad luck. I thought we were done for when Hikari said we should be made sailors so that we weren't stowaways anymore..." Izlude muttered as he repeatedly tapped the tips of his index fingers against each other.

"Cyrus was going to do that?!" Marina exclaimed. "I know he's old-fashioned, but...I'll have a word with him later, alright Izlude?"

"No, it's fine! Really! I don't want to get in trouble or anything." Izlude flailed.

"Alright, alright!" she giggled, "So how old are you?"

"I turned fifteen a month or so ago." he responded with a sigh, kicking the crate he was sitting on with the heels of his shoes.

"That's a little young to be out on your own. Where are your parents?" Marina questioned.

"They died when I was very little. I think my brother was six at the time..."

"Oh! I'm so sorry, I didn't know..." she responded, placing her hand over her mouth.

"They were caught in a barn fire I was told, trying to save some people. Don't worry. I don't miss them really. You have to know someone to miss them, right?" Izlude quietly pondered out loud.

"I understand that all too well. I was raised by my older sister on the outskirts of Port Tasuna. We didn't have much, but we got by with what we had. Then suddenly, without notice, she just kind of...disappeared shortly after I turned eighteen. I've been searching for her ever since. People tell me they've seen a woman with the same description every now and again, but every time I follow those leads, I hit dead ends." Marina said as she pulled a gun-shaped object from the holster at her side, "This was hers. I wasn't sure why she bought it. It might have been for our protection, but it was never fired once before she left."

"What is it?" Izlude asked curiously.

"You've never seen a beam-gun before?" she laughed, "Hmm, how to explain this...well, basically you pull back on the trigger here and these small, round, yellow orbs rapidly fly in the direction you point it. The orbs are dangerous and tear through pretty much anything they come into contact with."

Izlude gave her a confused look. Marina sighed and placed the beam-gun in his hands.

59

"Aim it out to the open sky and pull back on the trigger. You'll see."

Izlude nervously swallowed hard and held up the beam-gun, his arms shaking. He pointed it just above the entrance to the lower decks and shut his eyes.

Lars had spent a good hour waiting for the lounge to be opened up before he noticed Hikari's note to him letting him know the lounge was closed. He scratched his head, shrugged, and left. He paused for a moment as he was going down the stairs to the crew's quarters. Lars could hear some talking and laughter coming from the upper deck, so he decided to investigate. Shortly after heading up a few flights of stairs he recognized the voices of Izlude and Marina.

"Hey, Izlude, I- " Lars began as he emerged from the lower deck.

"Lars!!" he heard Marina shout.

Lars glanced in her direction and his eyes widened as he saw several yellow orbs flying straight in his direction. Lars cursed as he threw himself onto his stomach and shut his eyes. If he had reacted any slower, he was sure to have his travels cut short. Mere milliseconds after hitting the deck, the shots impacted the entrance. Lars cautiously glanced up at where his head had been only moments before and saw three charred indentations. Smoke could be seen wafting into the infinite sky above him and a loud sizzling noise broke the awkward silence.

"Bro! I'm so sorry! I didn't know you were going to be there!" Izlude apologized profusely, letting the beam-gun fall onto the wooden deck.

Marina hopped off of the crate she was sitting on and ran up to Lars. She knelt beside him and dusted off the back of his head.

"Are you okay?" she asked, concerned.

"Yeah, fine. Just startled me is all." Lars said as he stood up, trying to maintain his dignity.

"Oh thank Goddess, I thought you were a goner for sure." Marina sighed with relief.

She leaned backwards and sat on her heels. Marina looked over at Izlude staring at her beam-gun on the wooden deck and couldn't help but let out a chuckle.

"I should've told you to keep your eyes open." she shook her head with a smile.

"...I didn't know...I..." Izlude stammered quietly.

"Ah, it's fine. I'm still here and not a bloody mess all over the deck." Lars grinned, dusting himself off. "Besides, you'd have to clean up the carnage, Mr. Deck Swabber."

"I'm sorry, bro..." Izlude apologized again.

Marina sighed as she stood up and grabbed her beam-gun off the deck. She slid it into its holster and patted Izlude on the back. She glanced back at Lars and nodded to him. Lars understood Marina's silent pleading of him to change the subject and he placed his hand on his hip.

"Did I ever tell you about what we did in Drom for fun?" Lars asked.

"It doesn't sound like that village is a lot of fun. I mean, the only reason it's on the map is because technology is banned there. Most of the children in other towns are raised with the threat of being sent there if they did anything bad." Marina shrugged.

"Well let me tell you about our little group we founded..." Lars began.

"...and then Nak shouts, 'The chief just got an egg to the face, run for it!!' while dropping the whole basket of eggs we had been using! Kilik ends up slipping on the mess and wiping Grerr's and my feet out from under us. Then Nak turns around to come and help us up so we can run away from that ogre we have disguised as a chief but slips too! We caught such holy hell for that." Lars laughed as he reminisced about his activities with the Mercenaries.

"Oh my Goddess, I had no idea what sorts of mischief you could get into in such a rural area!" Marina laughed heartily.

"Oh that's nothing, one time Nak was-" Lars started to say.

"Hold it." Marina interrupted, her facial expression suddenly serious.

"Eh? What's wrong?" Lars asked, puzzled.

"The wind...something's not right at all. I need to see the captain!" Marina shouted as she quickly ran down the steps to a lower level.

"What's up, bro...?" Izlude asked, slightly nervous.

"I dunno," Lars said with a shrug. "Maybe she just didn't like Nak. Can't say I blame her."

"...But captain! I'm telling you! Something doesn't feel right..." Lars and Izlude heard Marina say through the metallic door leading to the navigation room.

"I trust your gut feelings more than any other sea-worthy sailor on the Sky Princess, but the fact of the matter is...there is absolutely nothing on our radar! The wind is the only thing that seems to have changed, and you know as well as I do that it happens often during this season!" Cyrus gruffly replied.

Lars turned to face Izlude and they both shrugged. Tenji quickly approached the navigation room door and unceremoniously shoved them aside. He then proceeded to enter the navigation room and shouted.

"Captain Cyrus! Y-You'd better have a look outside!" he yelled while jabbing a finger towards the upper deck.

Cyrus, Tenji, Marina, and two other sailors ignored Lars and Izlude and briskly brushed past them towards the upper deck. Lars folded his arms over his chest and shook his head.

"The next person who shoves me aside is going to get my

fist across their face-" Lars stopped suddenly as he was sent stumbling forwards.

"What the hell is wrong with..." Lars let his voice trail.

"Move it, pip-squeak!" Julius grunted as he forced his way past Lars.

Lars waited until Julius' back was to him before sticking his tongue out at the security officer. Izlude jumped in front of Lars and flailed his arms about, shaking his head at his brother. Lars shrugged and motioned for Izlude to follow him as he chased after Marina and the others. Upon emerging from the depths of the sky ship to the open air, Lars jumped backwards in surprise. Another sky ship was hovering beside the Sky Princess, casting a gigantic shadow over the cluster of sailors on the port side. They were staring up at it in a mixture of surprise and fear. Lars casually approached them.

"So, uh...what's going on?" he asked Captain Cyrus.

"We're cursed...I knew it was a mistake to keep you on board the ship...nothing can save us now..." Cyrus muttered in response.

"Captain! All of you! There are no such things as curses! Stop giving up and help me think of what to do!" Lars heard Marina yell.

"No curse? No one has emerged and there is no movement at all when we scanned it, meaning it's sailing by itself. It doesn't show up on radar, and it has stopped our ability to move. The ghost ship has arrived...We're cursed, Marina..." Captain Cyrus muttered.

"We could always blow it up." Lars joked to her.

"Our cannons are offline too, all of our systems have been affected. It's only a matter of time before our propulsion system stops working too..." Hikari replied.

"So, what? We'd just...drop?" Lars asked, frowning.

"Lars' idea might still work. If it's still hovering, it must still have working engines. We just need to board the ship and make them overheat until they explode." Marina said, "So who's coming with me?!"

"O-Onboard the ghost ship? There's no telling what sorts of demons or ghouls inhabit it..." Julius stammered without blinking.

Several of the sailors began muttering amongst themselves, their voices quivering. Many of them began to back away from Marina, much to her dismay. She withdrew her leather whip from her side and cracked it on the ground.

"You cowards! Is there no one brave enough to join me?" Marina growled.

"Hey, we'll go!" Lars smiled as he grabbed Izlude's hand and began waving it high.

"B-Bro?!"

"Even these two fledgling sailors are set to risk their lives for the good of this ship! I'm not going to ask again! Who's coming with me?" she shouted again.

"Hey! I said we would..." Lars frowned.

"No one else...?" Marina sighed in despair, "Fine. But if you two hold me back, promise me you'll come back to the ship with no hesitation."

Lars pumped his fist in the air and smiled. This was the kind of times he had dreamed of when he set his mind to leave Drom.

"Julius! Bring Lars and Izlude some weapons from the armory." Marina commanded, glancing down at Lars' broadsword.

"Hey, was that a jab at my sword? This baby's saved my life, I'm not going anywhere without it!" Lars replied, his hand grasping the hilt.

"Fine, but when it breaks, and it most likely will, don't be depressed. Just get Izlude a beam-gun or something, Julius." Marina sighed.

Izlude and Lars both shook their heads repeatedly at this notion. Izlude didn't want anything to do with a beam-gun for a very long time, and Lars wasn't up for being Izlude's accidental target practice again. Marina shook her head. If their situation hadn't been so dire, she definitely would have laughed at Lars and Izlude furiously shaking their heads. Hikari and Jahard suddenly came into view carrying a large, wooden plank, which they placed on top of the railings between the two sky ships. Lars approached the railing of the

Sky Princess and looked at the plank before looking down.

"Marina, Jahard and I will track your movements and guide you." Hikari nodded, tossing three communicator earpieces to Marina.

"Oh you've got to be kidding me." Lars muttered, feeling blasts of air hit his face and seeing the endless ocean several tens of thousands of feet beneath them.

Marina nimbly hopped onto the plank and motioned for Lars and Izlude to follow her. Lars cautiously placed a foot on the edge of the wooden, makeshift bridge and tested his weight on it before fully stepping onto it behind Marina. He then turned around and motioned for Izlude to do the same. Izlude gulped and closed his eyes. He thought of the last time Lars had asked him to tag along. He still had nightmares over the creature he had killed down in the depths of Drom.

Izlude opened his eyes and shook the memories from his head. He recalled what Captain Cyrus had said about no movement being detected inside as he placed a quivering foot on the edge of the plank.

No movement, nothing there, right...? he thought to himself.

He watched as Marina leapt off the plank and onto the wooden deck of the ghost ship. She turned around and nodded, waiting for Lars and Izlude to follow suit. Lars stuck his arms out as he traversed the two-foot wide bridge and turned around at the opposite railing to stick his arms out for Izlude to grab when he was close enough. He waited until his younger brother grasped his arm tightly before pulling him to the railing, where Marina was waiting directly below.

"Alright, we'll both jump onto the deck on the count of three, okay Izlude?" Lars shouted over the blasts of wind.

Izlude nodded nervously and prepared himself to jump.

"One..."

A quick glance behind him showed Izlude the still prominent dismay of the sailors on the Sky Princess. He shook his head and tried to focus on the task at hand.

"Two..."

Marina looked towards the bow of the ship. She wasn't

sure why she had agreed to bring them with her. Now that she thought of it, it made more sense to have just gone by herself. Maybe she was scared too, but didn't want to admit it. She shook her head. Now wasn't the time to worry. She put a little more pressure on her back foot to brace herself and felt the floor beneath her bend from her weight.

"Lars, no!!" Marina shouted with panic.

"Three!"

Lars and Izlude jumped off the railing and landed directly in front of Marina. Their feet remained on the deck for no longer than two seconds before the three of them broke through the wooden deck and plummeted into the dark abyss of the lower deck.

Jahard blinked and turned his body to face Hikari.

"Yep, we be doomed, kid." he stated.

"Come on! To the navigation room, we need to help them out!" Hikari dragged Jahard through the crowd of sailors still in shock.

"What be the point o' goin' to the navigation room if th' systems be down?" Jahard pointed out.

"Well you fixed the captain's vacuum robot, didn't you?" Hikari replied as they made their way towards the navigation room.

"That was a bucket o' bolts, this is a super computer!" Jahard protested while being shoved past the sliding, metallic door into the navigation room.

CHAPTER 10

Lars coughed and groaned as his sight began to clear from the sudden impact. He blinked a few times before looking around at his new surroundings. Izlude lay next to him, also dazed from the fall. Both of them were on a large, rotting coil of rope that seemed to have absorbed most of their landing. Lars rolled off the coil and stumbled onto his feet. He shakily readjusted to standing on something solid again.

"You alright, Izlude?" Lars asked.

"Yeah...I think so. Are you okay, bro?" Izlude said.

Lars stretched and nodded. He spotted Marina dusting herself off in the corner of the room and approached her. She bent over and picked her whip off the ground.

"I have no idea in Goddess' name where we are. But we probably overshot the engine room by at least three or four decks. I think we're in the cargo bay. They usually have the entire back of a sky ship dedicated to cargo storage." she said.

"Well how was I supposed to know we'd fall right through?" Lars said, throwing his arms in the air.

"Why'd you come along, anyways?" Marina sighed, unsure whether to be grateful or angry.

"...You ask why I came along? This is a fine time to ask now that we can't go back!" Lars replied.

Izlude sat up and tilted his neck back to look up at the small, circular opening they had fallen through. It seemed about the size of the moon on a cloudless night in Drom. He scratched his head and cautiously stood up on the coil of rope.

"Well we can't just stay here. Let's look around for a door. Watch your step and be careful, there's no telling what we'll come across." Marina ordered, "Put on these earpieces in case Hikari and Jahard try to contact us."

She tossed an earpiece to both Lars and Izlude who examined them before placing them inside their ears. A small wire immediately extended from the center of the earpiece, which wound itself around their cheeks before stopping over their mouths.

"Alright, let's get moving." Marina said.

"What the hell are you doing, Jahard?!" Hikari shouted as Jahard brought his fist against the control panel in front of the radar for the fourth time.

"That's how th' captain's robot be fixed! Y'asked me t'fix the navigation room, and this is what I be doin'!" Jahard yelled back.

"Oh for Goddess' sake..." Hikari groaned.

A flash of bright green filled the dimly lit room as the radar kicked back to life. Jahard stopped his fist inches from punching the control panel a seventh time. Hikari ran up to the screen and scanned it. Several blips onboard the ghost ship could be seen rapidly moving about the various decks.

"J-Jahard! I think they've got company! Quick! Beat the heck out of the communications systems!!" Hikari shouted, still monitoring the radar.

"Anyone else have the feeling that we're being watched?" Lars asked.

The three of them had discovered a door that led to the next deck of the sky ship and were currently walking up the steps.

"It's just your nerves. They scanned this ship. Remember? Nothing on radar." Marina replied.

"...What ghost shows up on radar?" Izlude nervously said.

Lars gripped the hilt of his broadsword cautiously making sure it was there if anything happened. The stairs eventually levelled off, revealing a significantly smaller room than the cargo room they had just left. Several oddly shaped holes were in the metallic floor and the only door that seemed to allow them to progress was on the other side.

"Watch out, you wouldn't want to fall any further. There's no telling where you might end up." Marina cautioned as she took a slightly larger-than-normal step over a hole.

"Don't need to tell me that twice!" Lars nervously chuckled as he followed her. "Stay close, Izlude."

After a short while of making their way towards the door, Lars spotted a shiny key on the ground in front of it.

"Hey Marina! Check this out." Lars said, approaching the key and picking it up.

"Lars! Watch it!" she shouted.

Marina threw herself against Lars sending the both of them sprawling against the floor. No sooner had she done so, a large pendulum tied to a rope swung swiftly through the air where Lars had been. It slammed against the metallic wall sending several shards flying in different directions.

"Geez!" Lars muttered, staring at the pendulum.

"I told you to be careful. It was a trap. That key probably isn't even real." Marina responded.

Sure enough, the key was broken in half from the fall. Lars looked at it further and determined it was made of a painted glass. He stood up and dropped it, letting it shatter on the ground. Marina approached the pendulum and got down on her hands and knees. She cautiously crawled beneath the pendulum's swing path and stood up directly in front of the door, which slid open upon detecting her presence. She took a step inside the next room, looked around, and turned to face Lars and Izlude. Lars had already crawled beneath it and was standing behind her.

"C'mon, Izlude! Nothing's going to happen, it's already been activated. Just crawl underneath it and you'll be fine!" Lars shouted words of encouragement.

Izlude swallowed and hesitantly placed his palms on the floor before crawling underneath the pendulum. The rope suddenly snapped, causing the pendulum to fall from the wall and become embedded in the floor. Izlude shut his eyes at the sound of the impact before carefully opening them and looking over his shoulder. The pendulum was a mere centimeter from the edge of his shoes.

"...Right. Let's move on!" Lars laughed anxiously as he helped Izlude back onto his feet. "Where are we now, Marina?"

"I'm not sure..." she replied.

She was standing in front of a large monitor located in the center of the room and was fiddling with the various controls in front of it.

"Lars, this isn't just any sky ship...it's a pirate sky ship. This is a cataloguing computer. It keeps track of all the sky ship's cargo, where they got it, how they got it, how much it's worth..." Marina's voice became inaudible as she read.

"P-Pirate sky ship...?" Izlude stammered.

"From the looks of things, the last contact this sky ship has had with anyone was...eighteen years ago." Marina read.

"Eighteen years ago? I guess that explains why there's no movement. They're all dead." Lars exclaimed with his hand on his chin.

"Lars...I don't like it here...let's just get out, please...?" Izlude pleaded.

"According to the log here, they came into contact with a sky ship called the Steel Falcon..." Marina continued.

"Did you say the Steel Falcon?" Lars responded quickly.

"Yeah, you've heard of it?" Marina asked, looking at him behind her shoulder.

"Dad used to talk about it all the time. He told me he used to be a medic on it." Lars answered.

"Dad worked on a sky ship?" Izlude softly asked curiously, forgetting for a moment their predicament.

"Yeah, a couple of years before you were born. He retired after you came into his life. Does it say what happened after they contacted them? Dad never told me about any sky pirates."

"It says that they stole some sort of Arcanian artifact. Here are some captain's logs." Marina said as she pushed a button.

"...The artifact in general seems to have caused a certain bloodlust in my men, more so than one should expect from men of their caliber. Many of them on occasion have burst into my quarters demanding to see it. In fear of a mutiny I have decided to place it in my vault along with my access card," a gruff, male voice echoed throughout the room.

"We'll be needing that access card to enter the engine room I'll bet." Marina said.

She pushed another button and the voice spoke again.

"Jahard! I see even more movement! They seem to be heading directly towards Marina, Lars, and Izlude! Hurry up!" Hikari frantically yelled from the radar screen.

"A'right, don't be gettin' in a twist." Jahard grunted as he kicked the metallic side of the communications console.

"Hold on guys..." Hikari muttered to the screen.

"This Arcanian artifact has brought a curse down on us. An engineer in the armory has programmed the sentries to kill us all in his search for it. The engineer himself was stupidly killed in crossfire and as a result cannot undo his programming. Me and a few men left are holed up in my quarters as I speak. We are running low on ammunition and energy. It's only a matter of time before the sentries reach their programmed destination. The object itself is safe. It remains in my vault, which is of Arcanian origins. It's not so easily destroyed and one must be in possession of another Arcanian artifact in order to open it. The Steel Falcon ... I wish we had never come across it." the voice echoed through sounds of beam-gun shots.

"Sentries?" Lars asked Marina, "What the heck is a sentry-"

A hovering, metallic disk crashing through the floor in front of them cut Lars off. Two rotating buzz saws horizontally stacked on top of each other popped out of its mouth, followed by a beam-gun emerging from the top lid.

"Marina! You've got company!" came Hikari's voice suddenly.

"Yeah? I hadn't noticed!" Marina shouted, whipping out her beam-gun and firing a shot at the sentry.

The sentry nonchalantly hovered slightly to the left, just enough to dodge it. Marina glared at it and fired two quick shots on each side of the hovering disc. The sentry seemed to ignore these, knowing full well their trajectories, and returned fire. Marina, Lars, and Izlude all dove in separate directions. The only difference being Marina did a simple roll and was back on her feet, whereas Lars and Izlude had to scramble to stand again.

"Damn it!" Marina cursed as she holstered her beam-gun and brought her whip out with a crack, "Now I'm angry!"

She instinctively snapped her whip back and cracked it in a horizontal path at the sentry. Its mechanical insides whirred almost like laughter as it moved just beneath the arc of the whip; however, before it could fire another beam-gun shot at Marina, it found it was missing its beam-gun. It spun around to face Lars who had just ripped it out of its socket.

"Well what do you know, these things just pop right off!" Lars commented.

The sentry, apparently angered, revved up its buzz saws and charged towards Lars. He flinched and whipped out his broadsword just in time to stop them from slicing his neck off. The rotating saws made a loud grinding noise against his metal blade but the broadsword remained steadfast in its position. Marina quickly brought up her beam-gun and aimed it at where the sentry's had been before pulling the trigger. The hovering robot made a squeal before it fell to the ground with a crash.

"Not even a scratch, that's some sword. Where'd you find it?" Marina panted, examining Lars' broadsword through curious eyes.

"In Drom before we hitched a ride. I haven't found anything that can damage it yet, not even a beam-saber." Lars shrugged.

"I think it might be Arcanian-" Marina began.

"There are more behind you! Turn around!" Hikari yelled.

Marina, Lars, and Izlude looked at each other before turning around to look behind them. Lars' mouth dropped at the sight of five sentries hovering in formation, their weapons activated.

CHAPTER 11

Beam shots danced around them as Lars, Marina, and Izlude dove for cover behind the massive cataloguing computer. Lars brought the beam-gun he had ripped off the first sentry up to his face and inspected its side before pulling the trigger casually.

"Lars! Aim at them not us!" Marina yelled at him as a beam shot blasted right past her.

"I didn't know it still worked!" he yelled back.

Lars stuck the beam-gun around the corner of the computer and blindly fired shots at the five sentries at the other end of the room. Izlude buried his face in his hands and tried to make his body as small a target as possible for the flying, metallic shrapnel that was cascading over the top of the cataloguing computer. Thoughts raced through his mind. If they decided to rush the cataloguing computer, the three of them would surely be killed.

"Damn it! Lars, I'm out!" Marina growled, holstering her beam-gun to her side.

"Out? These things run out of beam shots?" Lars asked.

"Yeah. You've been firing nothing for the past three minutes." Marina sighed.

"Hmm...Let's see if we got any."

Lars reached for a particularly large metal shard in front of him and looked at his reflection. He brushed a bit of his bright-red hair aside and leaned towards the edge of the cataloguing computer, took a deep breath and stuck the metal shard out of cover. All he could make out in the reflection was a cloud of dust, until a well-placed beam shot blasted his makeshift mirror out of his hand. Lars threw himself further behind cover and looked at Marina, shaking his head.

"Bro...? If these things run out of shots, they should be out soon, right?" Izlude questioned.

Lars and Marina looked down at Izlude and then at each other. Lars grinned and Marina shook her head.

"Those sentries are accurate as heck. You'd get shot to

pieces before you even had a chance to make them waste their shots!" Marina protested.

Lars tossed his beam-gun out to the side and watched it destroyed by a single beam shot before it hit the ground. He withdrew his broadsword from his belt and looked at it. His name was still engraved on the edge of the blade near the hilt.

"Accurate, but predictable." Lars nodded to his broadsword. "Don't fail me now!"

With that said, he leapt out of cover and watched as a beam shot headed straight for his head. He brought the blade of his broadsword in front of his forehead out of reflex and shut his eyes. Izlude's voice yelling, "Bro!" and Marina's yelling, "Lars!" seemed to mix in his mind. A loud, ringing noise echoed through his ears followed by the heat of an explosion. Lars snapped his eyes open just in time to see a sentry fall to the ground in flames. His broadsword seemed to have caused the beam shot to ricochet back to it. Lars brought his broadsword down and ran towards the remaining four sentries. Pain shot through his free arm as a stray beam shot grazed the outside of it.

Marina glanced over at Izlude and shook her head. She withdrew her whip and rolled out of cover. Marina then ran towards Lars who was trying to keep three pairs of saws from slicing him into bits. She saw the fourth sentry sneaking up behind Lars and cracked her whip at it. The beam-gun attached to the top of the sentry spun around. Marina grunted as she pulled her whip back and cracked it again, sending the sentry through the air to meet its demise against a wall. Lars swung his broadsword with both hands in a large arc and neatly sliced another sentry in half. The two remaining sentries paused for a moment before darting through a hole in the deck.

Lars looked around the room, waiting for another attack. Marina quickly put herself back to back with Lars and the two of them slowly spun around together, watching every corner of the room. A sudden sawing noise caused them to flinch. Lars glanced at Marina and she at him before looking down. Lars sighed as he forcefully brought his broadsword down and neatly buried it into the floor. A squeal pierced the room from the sentry that was attempting to saw through directly beneath them.

"Hikari! Any others?" Marina spoke into her microphone.

"No movement on radar, but they're still there." Hikari responded. "Watch out for any ambushes, Marina!"

"Understood." Marina glanced at Lars. "Lars, you're bleeding!"

"Just a graze, I'm fine." Lars nodded.

Marina nodded in response and approached the cataloguing computer. Smoke was billowing from the monitor where several beam shots had melted much of it. Marina attached her whip to her side and slammed her fist on the controls.

"Damn! We're going to have to find the captain's quarters without a map." she sighed.

"Marina, I can see some sort of unidentified energy source coming from a hundred yards to the north of your current position." Hikari's voice came, filled with static. "It seems to be interfering with...dar and..."

"Hikari?" Marina shouted into her microphone while tapping her earpiece. "Hikari!"

Silence filled the room. Marina shook her head and muttered something under her breath. She began walking towards the sliding door opposite the one they had entered. Lars bent over and picked Izlude up onto his feet before turning to face her.

"Where do you think you're going?" Lars asked her.

"I think if we take care of that energy source, we'll be able to get back into contact with Hikari," Marina responded. "Are you coming or staying behind?"

Lars looked down at a shaken Izlude and shrugged. He slid his broadsword into his belt and went to catch up with Marina.

"W-Wait for me, bro!" Izlude shouted as he snapped out of his shock. "I'm coming!"

Izlude sprinted through the sliding door towards his brother. He bumped into Lars immediately after the door slid open. Lars flinched and spun around with a hand on the hilt of his broadsword.

"Startled me." Lars muttered, slowly turning back around. "Well, we found the crew's quarters, Marina. Except ... which one's the captain's?"

Several hundred identical doors littered the long hall in front of them. Lars blinked as he regarded them all.

"It doesn't matter, we need to get Hikari back first. He's our eyes. We're blind without him." Marina replied.

"... Didn't Hikari say something about an energy source? What if it's the Arcanian artifact in the captain's safe?" Izlude tugged at Lars' shirt.

"Two birds with one stone if that's the case."

"Two birds...with one stone? Lars, I don't think I've heard that one before." Marina raised an eyebrow.

"Yeah, see, it's like a bonus. You get two birds for dinner using only one stone, as opposed to two stones." Lars explained.

"But how do you kill two birds with a single stone in one throw? It's impossible since after striking one of them, the stone would simply fall to the ground." Marina corrected him.

"It's just a saying! The point is, we should look for the captain's quarters first. I think Izlude might be on to something." Lars said, as he slammed his foot against the first door to his left.

It swung open revealing a dusty, metallic room with a single skeleton slumped in the corner. Lars apologized to it, reached into the room and pulled the door shut. Marina thought for a moment before opening the first door to her right. The room was empty except for a couple of hammocks hanging in opposite corners.

"This is gonna take a while." Lars sighed.

A surge of electricity ran through the sentinel's circuits. The dark room it occupied was suddenly lit a crimson red as it opened its sensors on its head.

"Running scans." its metallic voice pierced the silence. "Targets found. Retrieving prior orders...secure any and all Arcanian artifacts. Command understood. Activating rocket launchers and staccato machine beam-guns. Search and destroy mission beginning."

"Lars, found it yet?" Marina shouted, closing the fifth door she had opened.

When no response came, she approached the door Lars had last opened. Marina took a glance inside and saw Lars resting with his eyes closed in the solitary hammock inside. A broken skeleton lay on the ground beneath him, the only intact part being an arm with a bony hand still attached. Marina crept towards Lars incredibly silently, before crouching to pick up the arm. She slipped underneath the hammock and thrust the arm towards the roof before pulling it back down quickly. The hand of the arm tapped Lars' chest a couple of times. Lars opened his eyes and blinked a few times before yawning. He lazily looked down at the skeleton arm resting on his chest and analyzed it for a second before screaming loudly. He flailed violently before falling to the floor with a loud crash.

"That's not funny, Marina!" Lars shouted angrily.

"I thought it was." she laughed. "Serves you right, worrying me like that."

"Worried? You were worried about me?" Lars asked as he tilted his head to the side.

"...Guys? I think I found it..." Izlude's voice faintly entered the room from the hallway.

Lars got to his feet and dusted himself off. Marina rolled forward and sprung up on her legs before exiting the room with Lars. They could see Izlude staring inside a room a couple of doors north of them. Lars walked up to his little brother and patted him on the back.

"Good work!" Lars said, glancing into the room. "...Whoa! What happened here?!"

Several shattered skeletons were littered across the floor along with metallic pieces of what could only be sentries. The only skeleton intact was positioned in a faded, red, leather chair behind a large, metallic desk. A small safe remained positioned on the edge of the desk with several ancient symbols adorning it. No handle or anything resembling a possible way of opening it could be seen.

"The last stand..." Marina muttered as she entered.

"You know, if all these pirates wanted that artifact so badly...I wonder if it's worth something?" Lars pondered to himself.

"Well, it doesn't matter. We can't get this safe open without an Arcanian artifact ourselves." Marina commented, poking the metal safe with her finger.

Lars walked up to it and scanned it before withdrawing his broadsword and also poking it. He thought for a moment before opening his mouth. He paused for a moment with his mouth open and shut it again. Lars brought his broadsword back and swung it at the safe. It crashed against the safe with a solid clang. Lars shrugged and slipped the weapon back into his belt.

"Guess it's not Arcanian-" Lars began.

His voice was interrupted by a loud creaking noise coming from the safe. The wall facing the three of them suddenly slammed open onto the metal desk, revealing its contents. Lars stared at Izlude and then at Marina before folding his arms over his chest.

"You mean to tell me I had an Arcanian artifact this whole time and didn't know it?" Lars shook his head.

Marina stuck her hand inside the safe and withdrew a thin, plastic card. She slid it into her pocket before tilting her head.

"There's something wrapped in cloth in here. Lars, I think it's the artifact." Marina said.

Lars unfolded his arms and reached for the cloth. He grasped it and pulled it towards him.

"Whoa...it's cold!" Lars exclaimed.

He cautiously removed the cloth from the round object and let the cloth fall to the ground. A blinding bright light suddenly filled the room, blocking their sight from everything other than themselves in the room. The light quickly turned from white to a light brown before a map of the world emerged, projected on the walls around them.

"Marina?! What is this?!" Lars shouted, mesmerized.

"It can't be..." she muttered to herself.

"Marina!" Lars yelled again.

"It's a map..." Marina replied softly.

"Yeah, I can see that. But this isn't a normal map!"

"It's the map to the Crystal of Immortality." Marina stated.

CHAPTER 12

"You're wrong. You have to be. This map doesn't lead anywhere, there's no directions." Lars replied.

He had calmed himself down and set the round, orb-like artifact on the captain's desk. It still produced its eerie map, which dominated the quarters. Izlude extended his finger and pointed at a particular spot on a nearby wall.

"Brother! There's Drom!" he shouted happily.

"Lars, you don't understand. This is the map. It's almost as legendary as the Crystal of Immortality itself. It's not complete though. It's missing pieces." Marina explained as she inspected the various locations shown.

"Not complete? If this is what it does when it's missing parts, I'd hate to see it at one hundred percent!" Lars exclaimed.

"No, no. They say you need to find the first piece, which will lead you to the second piece, and then so on and so forth until you reach the Crystal of Immortality. No one's ever had both the first piece and the map before."

"Why would anyone hide something and then make a map for it, only to make it nearly impossible to find it?" Lars protested.

"Well, if you worked that hard on an artifact that could grant immortality," Marina continued. "I'm sure you wouldn't want it to be completely forgotten and eventually lost. Maybe it's the grand mage's way of filtering out weak people."

"Sounds like some wild goose chase to me." Lars frowned.

"Wild...goose chase?" Marina blinked.

"It's an old saying from Drom, you see-"

"Never mind. We need to toast this sky ship, we'll talk about this later." Marina commanded.

Lars snatched the artifact off the desk and tossed it in his pocket after covering it with the cloth again. Izlude tugged on his shirt and Lars glanced down at him.

"Uh...bro? Is it safe in your pocket?" Izlude meekly asked. "I mean if it's old it could be fragile..."

"Psh, my broadsword has been shot at, sawed at, and slashed at. It's still good to go! They just don't make 'em like they used to, I guess." he shrugged, patting his slightly bulging pocket.

"Hikari, it's Marina. Can you hear me?" Marina shouted into her headset. "Damn...We'll need to find the engine room ourselves, that map is causing the interference. Help me search the captain's desk here, there must be something."

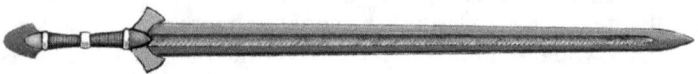

A lone sentry whirred through the air towards the newly activated sentinel. Upon approaching its massive back, the sentry darted in front of its face and spun its inside gears, creating a loud high-pitched squeal.

"Intruders detected on deck gamma. Priority of orders changed. First priority: locate targets and terminate them. Second priority: recover any and all Arcanian artifacts. Arming activated weaponry."

"Y'know, it's a good thing you found the blueprint of the sky ship when you did, Marina." Lars said. "This place gives me the heebie-jeebies."

"The whats?" Marina asked with a raised eyebrow.

"Well, it's sort of, ...kind of... I can't even begin to explain it." Lars tried to answer.

Marina had poked around the captain's desk, looking in all the drawers for any direction at all as to where the engine room was. After several minutes of watching her search, Lars had walked up to a nearby trash bin and punted it. The bin had flown through the air eventually hitting Izlude in the back of the head. Izlude had shouted in shock and flailed as he fell forward onto his stomach. Lars had immediately rushed up to him and helped him back on his feet.

"Sorry, Izlude. You know what happens when I get bored." Lars had apologized with a shrug.

The trash that had been inside the bin had floated lazily towards the ground before a crumpled, blue sheet had landed on Lars' face, blocking his vision. Marina had tilted her head and quickly snatched it off Lars.

"Lars, you genius! This is the ship's blueprint! Here, help me spread this out." Marina had happily commanded as she wiped the contents of the drawers off the desk with her arm.

Now, Lars was leaning against a nearby wall while Marina tinkered with a large computer in front of three floating spheres encased in metal. They produced an eerie, blue glow that enveloped the room. Izlude was sitting beside him, his legs crossed, feeling exhausted from all the stress and nervousness he had been feeling the whole time quite sure they were going to get ambushed at any moment. But Lars just brushed those thoughts aside whenever Izlude brought them up.

"Well, as soon as I figure out how to overheat the engine we'll be out of here. I've swiped the captain's access card, but it still wants a password." Marina sighed. "And unfortunately, I'm not as gifted in hacking computers as some people."

"Marina, how much time would we have to get back before it would be too late?" Lars asked, kicking himself off the back wall and walking towards the engine.

"Ideally? Five minutes. But if it falls slowly, we might have seven." she replied.

"I have an idea. You know how this...eh...thing works, right?" Lars asked, pulling out his broadsword.

"Yeah, why?"

"What if we damage the part that cools the engine?" Lars mused.

"It's worth a try. I'm not making any progress with this terminal. It's that large cable running along the ground there. Have at it." she nodded.

Lars brought his broadsword up behind his head before swinging it heavily at the cable. His blade neatly sliced it in half, causing a voice to emerge from a nearby speaker.

"Core temperature rising. Engineering report to engine room as soon as possible." the voice dully announced.

"You did it, Lars! Now let's get out of here!" Marina yelled. "The stairs up to the top deck of the ship aren't too far from here."

The three of them quickly left the engine room and made their way back to the pirates' quarters' hallway. Izlude's hairs on the back of his neck prickled as he felt someone or something watching them. He was about to tell Lars but thought better of it. Lars would simply toss the idea aside as usual. A sudden vibration emerged from the walls of the sky ship.

"We need to pick up the pace. If we continue up this hallway we'll reach the stairs." Marina gasped, pausing to catch her breath.

"Uh, Marina? What are those red orbs floating in the dark?" Lars asked as he squinted in the direction they had come from.

"Red orbs...?" she replied.

Marina turned around and also squinted into the darkness. The orbs were slowly getting larger until their owner finally emerged from the darkness fifty feet away from the trio. Marina's eyes grew wide as she realized what it was.

"Sentinel!!" she shouted.

The massive robot barely fit in the halls, but that didn't stop it from raising its highly destructive arms and aiming them at Lars, Marina, and Izlude. On each arm, two rockets were stacked on top of eight barrels ready to rapidly fire beam shots at any target it chose.

"Arcanian artifacts detected. Target acquired." the sentinel's metallic voice echoed throughout the hall.

"Lars! Run!" Marina yelled as she grabbed onto Izlude and gave him a hard push towards the stairs opposite the sentinel.

"Oh, geez!!" Lars shouted.

He had just realized what the sentinel had meant, pivoted

his front foot and sprinted behind Izlude and Marina. The sentinel brought its targeting reticule up from Lars and projected it to the roof of the hallway in front of him. It knew that it had a higher statistical chance of retrieving the artifacts by preventing Lars from running further than shooting directly at him. The sentinel pointed an arm in line with its reticule causing the arm's mechanical elbow to lock. With that done, it quickly fired a single rocket at its chosen target. Marina turned her neck to look over her shoulder at Lars when she saw the rocket fly out of the sentinel's arm.

"Lars! Duck!" Marina shouted frantically.

The last Marina and Izlude saw of Lars was him throwing himself on the ground, dodging the rocket but not the resulting debris that crashed with a large cloud of dust causing Marina and Izlude to hack violently. Both remained in shock. Izlude fell to his knees in front of the rubble. He couldn't blink if he wanted to.

"Brother...?" he quietly said to the giant mass of crushed metal sealing them from the sentinel.

"Lars!" Marina shouted. "Are you alright?! Answer me!"

The sky ship rocked sharply, throwing Izlude onto his hands from his kneeling position. He watched as a few tears dripped from his face and created small, clean spots in the dust. Marina wrapped her arms around his waist and pulled him to his feet. Izlude immediately began to flail while desperately trying to break her grip.

"We've got to get out of here or he'll have died in vain! Come on, Izlude!" Marina yelled at him.

"No! I'm staying here! I'm not leaving my brother!" Izlude cried.

"I know he's your family but damn it, Izlude! Do you think he'd want you to throw your life away?!" Marina shouted in response, "Please...I'm not going to lose the both of you...it would be my fault for letting you come with me."

"Marina..." Izlude quietly spoke.

He conceded and let her drag him towards the stairs. After climbing several flights of metallic stairs they reached a door which Marina promptly kicked open with a well-placed

85

sidekick. The distance between them and the bridge to the Sky Princess was a great one. Marina took a deep breath and looked at Izlude.

"No crying now. Save your energy." Marina said. "Let's go!"

The two sprinted towards the bridge. Marina was constantly looking around for any signs of a sentry waiting for them in ambush as they ran. She stopped looking when she realized that since they were not in possession of the map or an Arcanian artifact anymore, they were no longer targets. They just needed to make it back to the bridge.

She could see Hikari, Jahard, Captain Cyrus and the various other sailors she knew motioning for them to hurry onto the ship. Marina felt a large pain in her side and winced as she pushed herself to run more. Izlude's shallow breathing was also causing his body some discomfort but his mind was still back down below with Lars. Upon reaching the plank, Marina noticed how unlevel it was in bridging the gap between the two sky ships. She quickly leaped on top of it and extended a hand for Izlude to grab. He did so and the two of them managed to stumble onto the deck of the Sky Princess just as the plank fell towards the ocean below. Hikari and Jahard managed to catch Marina and Izlude respectively before they fell on the wooden deck.

"Where's Lars?" Hikari shouted over the wind.

"...He didn't make it." Marina responded while looking back at the pirate sky ship.

Izlude pushed himself away from Jahard and ran up to the railing. With tears in his eyes he watched as the pirate sky ship slowly tilted forwards. Marina pulled him towards her and held his head close to her shoulder.

"I didn't think Lars be the type o' person t'die that easy." Jahard said to Hikari.

"If there hadn't been interference, I might've been able to help." he responded darkly. "I'm to blame for this."

The sailors removed their helmets and placed them on their chests and in respect for Lars' sacrifice, lowered their heads. Marina wiped her eyes with the back of her free hand.

"Lars...you can't be dead, can you?" she said inaudibly.

CHAPTER 13

Lars rolled over onto his back and groaned. His ears were still ringing loudly from the explosion a short time ago. He thought he might have heard Izlude and Marina talking but he was temporarily deafened. He coughed as he accidentally inhaled the surrounding dust. Lars brought his shirtsleeve up to his nose and mouth and stood up. After examining the debris perfectly sealing him from the other end of the hallway and his eventual freedom, he sighed. Lars' legs suddenly staggered as he felt the pirate sky ship tilt downwards.

"Gotta find another way out." Lars coughed to himself.

The dust in the hallway was so thick that his vision was reduced to only a foot in front of him. After taking a few dazed steps he walked face-first into a large, metallic object.

"...the heck?" Lars asked no one in particular as he rubbed his nose.

Large, red orbs suddenly flashed in front of Lars' face causing him to jump straight back.

"You're still alive?!" Lars gasped.

He fumbled for his broadsword while squinting through the haze. The dust finally settled on the ground and Lars brandished his weapon in front of him, preparing for any movement on the sentinel's part. They stared at each other for a short while before the sentinel spoke.

"Obtain Arcanian artifacts through any means necessary." the sentinel stated again, raising its arm at Lars.

Lars' eyes widened and after frantically looking around for somewhere to take cover, he prepared himself to make a last charge. The sentinel's staccato machine beam-gun started to glow yellow as it warmed itself up before firing rounds at Lars. Before it could unleash a single beam shot a large, metallic chunk from the roof fell with a clang on top of its head. Its red eyes fizzled slightly before returning to their usual brightness.

"Retrieving prior orders...retrieving prior orders...no prior orders given, requesting new orders."

"Amnesia?" Lars raised an eyebrow.

"Order 'Amnesia' not viable order, please reword order." the sentinel replied.

"Alright then...get me the hell out of here!" Lars shouted.

"Order 'get me the hell out of here' understood. Priority of order?"

"Priority?! Top!" Lars yelled at the robot.

"Creating alternate route." it stated after examining the debris.

The sentinel raised both arms towards the eastern wall right next to Lars. He cursed and dove behind the massive robot to protect himself from the shrapnel. The heat of the detonation blasted against Lars' face. He shut his eyes and pressed his back against the cool, metal back of the sentinel. It suddenly began to walk east causing Lars to fall onto his back. He picked himself up and stared at the newly-created hole in the wall.

"Hey! Wait up!!" Lars shouted.

He ran up to the sentinel and climbed onto its back. Lars' hands grasped its shoulders while his feet were turned sideways on the curve of its lower back. Every step shook Lars and he had a hard time holding on.

"Can't you be a little more graceful?" Lars complained.

The sentinel seemed to ignore him. Shortly after taking a few dozen steps, it fired another rocket into a nearby wall. Lars felt a pain in his arm and looked down to where the sentry's stray shot had grazed him earlier. He was bleeding more but he knew that now wasn't the time to think about it. The sentinel stepped through what was left of the wall and entered what could only be the pirate sky ship's armory. Lars saw various machines and weapons that he could only dream of how they functioned. A large explosion rocked the pirate sky ship immensely.

"Engines have been destroyed. Estimated time until impact: two minutes." the familiar dull voice echoed throughout the sky ship.

"Did you hear that?! Get us to the upper deck!" Lars commanded frantically.

The sentinel stepped onto a nearby platform that automatically began rising rapidly towards the ceiling. Lars craned his neck up and watched as they came closer and closer to it. Shortly after starting their ascent, the roof began to part open until a large, square hole was created. The platform abruptly stopped after levelling itself with the upper deck. A quick glance around caused Lars to panic. The Sky Princess was several dozens of feet above the pirate sky ship. He squinted and saw the sailors above him. They seemed to be saluting the pirate sky ship.

A sudden cranking noise roared through the wind and Lars saw a large cannon protrude from the middle of the pirate sky ship's wooden deck and aim right at him. The sentinel quickly fired two rockets destroying the cannon but not before the canon had fired a single rocket. The sentinel took the rocket square in the chest. Lars was thrown off the sentinel and he landed on the wooden planks with a thud. He stood up and approached the pile of metal shrapnel that used to be the sentinel and picked up a particularly large one.

"Alas, poor sentinel. I knew it well." Lars mused.

He heard a large swarm of whirring noises and looked up curiously. Several sentries were converging on his location, their saw blades whirring and their beam-guns aimed.

"Poor Lars! I knew him well!!" Lars exclaimed as he threw the chunk of metal at a nearby sentry.

The sentry was unable to dodge in time and it fell to the ground with a clank.

"There was nothing you could do, Marina...stop blaming yourself so harshly." Hikari told her.

"Then who should I blame? It was my decision to let him come with me!" she yelled at the bartender.

"Hey! Look at th' ship! Lars be on top o' the pirate ship!"

Jahard shouted happily.

"What?!" Marina replied, letting go of Izlude.

She ran up to the railing and looked down below. She could see Lars surrounded by sentries desperately fending them off.

"Someone get a rope!" she yelled before cupping her hands beside her mouth. "Lars!! Hold on!"

"Marina! Th' only rope we be havin' is th' one beside th' bow." Jahard replied shortly after.

"It'll have to do." she decided. "Lars! Get to the bow of the pirate ship! We'll lower a rope!"

"Get to the bow? How am I supposed to do that?!" Lars shouted back.

"Improvise!" Hikari answered.

Lars glanced down at the sentry he had first sent crashing to the ground and then at the slope of the pirate sky ship as it was falling before an idea popped into his head. He jumped on top of the sleek sentry and started to accelerate rapidly down the sky ship.

"This has got to be the smartest idea I've ever had, or the stupidest!!" Lars shouted in panic as he flailed his arms.

Another explosion occurred from within the pirate sky ship causing several wooden planks to protrude upwards at an angle. Lars blinked as he realized he was unable to steer the sentry around them. He yelled while the sentry hit the makeshift ramp and sent him sailing through the air, only to land on the deck again with the sentry below his feet. Lars wiped his forehead with the back of his arm. He was almost at the bow. He could see several sailors on the Sky Princess holding a thick rope, waiting for him to grab a hold of it. Lars heard some more whirring and several more sentries burst through the floor.

"You've gotta be kidding me!" Lars exclaimed.

He swung his broadsword at the first sentry and cleaved it neatly in half as he passed by it. The other sentries darted towards the bow and started to fire at Lars. He deflected one beam shot but it ricocheted off his blade and hit the sentry he was riding causing Lars to be sent flying off of it. He tumbled onto the ground and quickly picked himself up. He would have to run the rest of the way.

"The pirate ship is too low! The rope's not long enough to reach it!" Cyrus roared. "We need a back-up plan, Marina!"

"He'll make it." Marina responded.

Lars ran forward while looking at the rope. It was six feet from the bow and he was positive he would be unable to make the jump, especially with sentries firing at him. He noticed two sentries hovering in front of the rope, one a couple of feet lower than the other and closer to Lars. Lars took a deep breath and sprinted towards them. He leapt over two beam shots and placed a foot on top of the first sentry before jumping onto the next. The first sentry overcompensated for Lars' weight and the moment he left it, the sentry soared up and exploded under the belly of the Sky Princess. The second sentry protested by grinding its gears in order to stay hovering.

"W-Whoa!" Lars shouted as he looked down at the endless ocean far below him.

He had one shot to grab the rope. If he missed, it would be the end of him. He took another deep breath, slid his broadsword in his belt, and jumped for the rope. He extended his arms to catch it and managed to grasp it with his hands.

Lars breathed a sigh of relief as the sailors began to pull him up. A large blast of fire shot up from the pirate sky ship causing the Sky Princess to rock. Lars' grip faltered and he slipped off the rope. A large hand shot past the railing and grabbed Lars' arm.

"I've got you, Lars!" Julius said. "Welcome back."

Lars was swiftly yanked over the edge of the railing and onto the wooden deck of the Sky Princess where Hikari, Jahard and the other sailors were cheering and laughing in relief.

"Almost missed my flight!" Lars grinned.

"Brother!!" Izlude cried out.

Izlude ran forwards and hugged his brother around the waist. Fresh tears were streaming down his face, mostly in joy that Lars wasn't dead. Lars shook his head and patted Izlude on top of his. Marina approached him looking angry.

"Oh, hey Marina! I see you got out safely-"

Marina slapped Lars hard on the cheek and stared at him. Lars flinched in shock and rubbed his face.

"What the heck was that for?!" Lars groaned.

"Never worry me like that again! Ever!!" Marina shouted at him before hugging him tightly.

"M-Marina?" Lars stammered.

She let go of her embrace and looked at him. Lars looked back before sticking his hands in his pockets to try and dodge the awkward situation. He felt a round, cold object in his pocket and his eyes brightened. He withdrew the clothed map and grinned at Marina and Izlude. Marina's eyes widened and she shook her head slightly to avoid detection. Lars quickly got the idea that no one else on board the sky ship should know of it and slid it back into his pocket.

"Lars! You be bleedin' all over th' deck! Ya need t'get to th' infirmary!" Jahard said.

"I'm fine! It's only a...little...wound..." Lars began to mutter before collapsing onto the deck.

CHAPTER 14

"Did you have fun with your little escapade on the pirate sky ship?" she giggled in Izlude's ear.

Izlude was in the white room again. He turned his head around, looking for the source of the voice as he always did but, yet again, didn't find it.

"Fun...that wasn't fun..." Izlude quietly responded.

"My apologies, Izlude, your mother would have thought it was." the voice sighed.

"My mother was a farmer! She wouldn't have enjoyed that at all and honestly, I think it's very cowardly to hide yourself from me! This is just a dream, I should have complete control, whoever you are!" Izlude roared.

"Do you think this to be a dream? Perhaps it is, perhaps it isn't. How are you supposed to know which is the dream and which is reality? Maybe Lars Nokuten or Marina Jayd don't really exist. Just a thought, Izlude." came the answer.

"Was that the adventure you told me about?" Izlude asked after a few moments of silence.

"That was only the beginning, the Arcanian prophecies dictate that many more challenges litter your path to greatness."

"Prophecies...? Path to greatness...? What do you mean?"

"I'm sorry, our time is being cut short again. If you wish to know the truth, seek out an old friend of your mother's near Port Tasuna. Goddess speed, Izlude." her voice trailed off again.

"The ship has movement again, so we'll be in Port Tasuna in a week or so. Captain Cyrus says we burned a little too much fuel but we should make it." Marina explained to Lars.

Lars was stretched out on a bed with a white bandage

wrapped around his upper left arm where he had been shot.

"I wish they'd just let me out of here already. I've been cooped up here for a couple days now." Lars complained.

"Captain Cyrus wants you to rest after that whole pirate sky ship ordeal, he says that you deserve it." she replied.

"Yeah, maybe, but I'd rather spend it lounging around in other areas of the sky ship. And besides I'm starving! You know how terrible the food they've been giving me lately is?" Lars shouted.

"I wouldn't yell too loudly about that..." Marina cautioned.

"And why not?! It tastes like mud!" Lars protested.

"Because Julius has been cooking for you the past few days," Marina answered. "The cook has been sick."

"...Well now that I think about it, it's not that bad..." Lars muttered.

He sat up and withdrew the Arcanian map orb from behind his pillow. Marina took a few steps to the stool beside Lars' hospital bed and gently sat down on it.

"So what're you going to do with your map?" Marina asked, running her fingers through her hair. "You could make a lot of credits selling it."

"Sell it? I'm not going to sell it! I'm going after the artifact!"

Marina choked on her own saliva and coughed herself off the stool and onto the infirmary floor. She coughed for a few more seconds before grabbing onto the metal framework of the bed and pulling herself back to her feet.

"Are you alright?" Lars asked, concerned.

"Lars...thousands, maybe tens of thousands, of people have died trying to find the Crystal of Immortality. It's not worth throwing your life away for..." Marina answered.

"It's not throwing my life away. When I left Drom I was looking for excitement, adventure, anything other than living a normal, boring life. Wouldn't you rather die on an adventure than of old age thinking of the endless possibilities you missed?" Lars swung his legs over the side of the infirmary bed to look at Marina.

Izlude cautiously pushed open the door to Lars' room and

95

walked inside. He hadn't heard past what Lars had just said and wasn't sure if he should be involved in the conversation. Marina glanced at Izlude as he carefully took a few steps into the room and nodded to him.

"And what about Izlude? Have you decided Izlude's fate too? He's a boy, Lars. He'll just be in danger. We barely made it out of the pirate sky ship in one piece, let alone crawling fifty dungeons looking for map pieces." she said.

"...D-Danger? What does she mean, brother?" Izlude stammered.

"We're going after the Crystal of Immortality as soon as we land in Port Tasuna." Lars stated simply.

"W-We are?!" Izlude blinked.

"Yeah, you, me and Marina." Lars nodded to his brother.

"I can't...I'm sorry, Lars." Marina said as she stood up and walked towards the door.

"Why not?" Lars tilted his head.

But Marina was already gone. Lars shook his head and hopped onto his feet. His picked up his broadsword, nodded to it, and slid it under his belt. Lars then stuck his hand out and ruffled Izlude's light brown hair.

"Guess it's just us, Izlude. Come on. Let's see if we can't rustle up some grub. I'm starving." Lars frowned.

Izlude reached out and pinched a bit of Lars' skin on his arm. Lars jumped in surprise and pain and rubbed the spot where he had been pinched.

"What the heck was that for, Izlude?!" Lars scolded.

"Just checking if what someone said to me was real..." Izlude replied.

"Well yeah, it's real. You pinch someone, it hurts." Lars shook his head.

Several days later, Port Tasuna was almost in view of the Sky Princess. They had spent the remaining days aboard the sky ship performing various tasks for the passengers on board. As a result, Lars and Izlude had earned a decent amount of credits in tips, nothing too fancy but not small either. They had enough red bills of currency to pay for several meals. Lars and Izlude often talked excitedly with Marina about Port Tasuna and what was located there. She seemed to have accepted the fact that Lars wouldn't give up his impossible notion and decided she had might as well support him.

"Port Tasuna is just that, a port for sky ships. But you can get a lot of shopping done there too. You should go buy some better clothes while you're in town, yours are looking a little shabby." Marina had said three days earlier.

"Shabby? I've only had this shirt for four years!" Lars had retorted, looking down at his faded green shirt.

"Fine, fine. But you're definitely going to want to go to Heaven's Fist if you're still thinking about doing you-know-what. You'll need to watch your back though, a lot of shady characters hang around there and there are plenty of under-the-table deals. You might get some information on the first piece for the right price." she had whispered as Tenji walked past them in the cafeteria.

"Black market, eh?" Lars excitedly asked.

"Bro..." Izlude said quietly, "Isn't that illegal...?"

"Since when has that ever stopped us?" Lars chuckled.

Lars and Izlude were standing on the upper deck of the Sky Princess among the other sailors, passengers and Captain Cyrus. The sun was shining brightly and the sky ship was slowly dipping its way towards a large building with the text "Hanger 432" written on a metallic door that covered the entire wall facing them. The building seemed to be protruding out of what appeared to be a large dome with an opaque roof. Upon reaching a closer distance to the hanger's wall, the metallic door began to slowly slide up until it revealed a mechanic's workshop of sorts. Several shiny robots parted as the Sky Princess lowered herself cautiously inside Hanger 432 until metallic clamps slid out of the floor and latched onto the bottom of the sky ship. A ramp then folded out of the starboard railing and flipped down at a forty-five degree angle before resting on the floor of the hanger. The robots that had parted only moments before began to furiously dart around the sky ship, inspecting it with determination. The passengers then began to make their way down the newly created departure ramp with several pieces of luggage each. Once the last passenger touched the ground, Captain Cyrus turned to face his sailors.

"Your bank accounts have all had your credits wired to them for this trip." Cyrus growled. "But don't be spending it all on cheap women and cheaper alcohol!...is what I'd like to say, but we all know you're going to be doing it anyways. Go have a good time, lads. We depart tomorrow morning at nine o'clock. If you're not here, you'll be left behind!"

The sailors all saluted and made a wild dash towards the ramp, leaving Lars and Izlude coughing in their dust. Marina shook her head and laughed heartily at their expressions. Hikari quickly approached Lars and shook his hand vigorously.

"Lars! It was a pleasure working with you. You should stowaway more often!"

"Heh, take care, Hikari." Lars nodded and Hikari ran after the sailors with Tenji.

Jahard waved to Lars and Izlude and smiled a slightly toothless grin before doing the same. Captain Cyrus took a few thundering steps towards the brothers from Drom before nodding.

"Sorry to do this, lads, but I have to fire you. You're no longer sailors, so go and do what your hearts want. Good luck on your travels and if you ever need passage on the Sky Princess you're more than welcome to work for me again and get it for free." Cyrus nodded. "Watch your last step at the bottom of the ramp."

DUNGEON CRAWLERS Episode 1

Lars nodded in reply and motioned for Izlude to follow him. His younger brother did so with Marina slightly behind him. Upon reaching the bottom of the ramp, Lars stumbled as he got reacquainted with the sense of being on solid ground again. When he regained his footing, he looked up and was astounded at the sight of Port Tasuna. His misstep had sent him just outside the open entrance to Hanger 432.

Izlude felt extremely overwhelmed at the hundreds of tall buildings that littered the port among the various hangers. The smell of a delicious food wafted in front of Izlude, causing his stomach to growl in protest. He glanced around curiously at the various structures, trying to discover its source but was unsuccessful. Lars was suddenly strongly shoved aside by a couple walking down the sidewalk.

"H-Hey! What's the big idea?!" he protested.

"Stop gawking, ya country bumpkin!" came the male's response.

"Friendly people you have here, Marina." Lars folded his arms across his chest.

She sighed and shook her head at Lars with a smile. Marina knew that even though Lars had no knowledge of what he would consider a futuristic setting, he would make it. She just wished that she could be there to guide him when things proved difficult. But that choice remained out of her hands.

"Well Lars, I guess this is it, huh." Marina said quickly as something seemed to catch her eye in the crowded street.

"You're leaving already? C'mon, Marina!" Lars protested.

"It can't be helped, I have...things I have to attend to. Tell you what, if you need anything, you can always stop by my cabin." she distractedly explained.

"...Your cabin?"" Izlude curiously asked.

"I don't like living in the helter-skelter of Port Tasuna. My sister and I used to live together in this cabin at the top of Burgalow Hill on the outskirts of town. When she disappeared, I never bothered to sell it...just in case she came back, you know? Anyways, I really have to get going. I'll...see you later." she muttered before breaking into a jog to the east.

"Huh. Wonder what that was about?" Lars scratched his head, as she was lost in the crowd of people.

"She didn't mention she had to do anything when we were on the Sky Princess..." Izlude quietly pondered.

"Eh...let's just find this Heaven's Toe." Lars replied.

"I thought it was called 'Heaven's Fist'...?" Izlude asked nervously.

"What's the difference?" Lars shrugged, his bright red hair blowing in the wind.

CHAPTER 15

"No minors allowed!!" the orcish bouncer bellowed at Lars.

The green, large, wart-covered monster stood guarding the entrance of the Heaven's Fist sushi bar. Lars gulped as he brought his gaze from the orc's chest, craning his neck back to look into his fiery eyes.

"Do you by any chance know a sailor named Julius on the Sky Princess? You have a lot in common with him." Lars chuckled nervously.

"No minors allowed! Kid no enter." the orc growled, a broken husk protruding out of his mouth and over his upper lip.

"Fine, fine. Izlude, wait for me out here, alright? Try not to bother the nice man...er..." Lars trailed off.

"Grunk no man! Grunk is orc! Man pay Grunk for protection because man weak!" came his low growl again.

Izlude sighed and sat down a few meters away from the bouncer. Lars looked at his younger brother and shrugged before approaching Grunk.

"Hey, Grunk..." Lars whispered with five red credits in hand, "Watch him for me, will ya? Make sure he doesn't get into any trouble."

"Trouble? Grunk watch for five minutes. One credit, one minute." he replied, grabbing the credits with a meaty fist.

Lars nodded in appreciation and made his way past the orcish bouncer into Heaven's Fist. The building itself hadn't been hard to find but it had taken several people to get the proper directions. Since Lars observed that the people in Port Tasuna seemed like they were all on their own agendas and wouldn't stop for many things, he changed his direction-asking tactics drastically each time. They ranged from him being a drunkard who had left his things in Heaven's Fist to being an amnesiac looking for a way to jog his memory.

The darkness seemed to consume Lars as he glanced about the shady sushi bar. He could see several occupied tables in the various corners of the room with extremely dim lamps above them. The people glanced in his direction casually before shaking their heads and going back to their conversations. Several waiters were strolling around the room, taking orders and placing them quickly on the tables before leaving as fast as they could. From what Marina told him, the waiters preferred not to hear anything of what was being said on the risk of overhearing the wrong thing and losing their lives over it. Lars took a few steps ahead and approached the bar in the center of the room. He casually grabbed a seat on a nearby barstool and waited for the bartender to notice him.

"Alright, what can I get for you?" he asked without turning around.

"Uh...milk I guess." Lars replied.

"...Milk? Why the hell would you order milk at a bar? You know what, never mind, coming up." the bartender sighed.

Shortly afterwards a tall, frosty glass of milk was placed on the counter. Lars extended a hand and took a large gulp of it before placing it back down.

"It's your reputation, not mine." he shrugged. "Three credits."

Lars placed three of the red notes on the counter and the bartender snatched them up before departing to another customer further down the wood. Lars sighed and took another sip of his milk before letting his eyes caress the sushi bar. He understood what Marina had said about the place being filled with shady characters. Several of the people sitting had dark cloaks draped over their forehead or sat back in certain positions so that the light never revealed more than their mouths. His ears were soon drawn to a nearby conversation coming from behind him. To avoid suspicion, Lars casually faced the bar again and pretended to be occupied with his drink while he listened in.

"So yeah, I got this tip from an acquaintance of mine that there's a ton of credits to be made looting Tekky's Tower to the north of town." a gruff, male voice said.

Lars froze and thought quietly to himself at the mention of

Tekky's name before returning to the conversation.

"You actually went to that crazy engineer's tower? Are you nuts?!" his companion responded.

"I don't think he's really crazy, just eccentric. I mean, no one's met the guy in what, thirteen years? He sends his robots out to get all of his things. Anyways, let me finish! You're sidetracking me." the first one protested. "So I go inside the entrance and just when I'm thinking the place is abandoned, I get waylaid by these crazy robots! I'm not talking about sentries or sentinels. These were things he must've built himself. My beam shots were bouncing off them and everything!"

"So...w-what'd you do?"

"Psh, I ran for it. I ran down one of the halls and I lost them after a bit, so I continued looking for anything of value. That's when I saw it," the thief suddenly lowered his voice, "it was definitely Arcanian. I think it was you-know-what."

"How do you know that I know what 'you-know-what' is?" scoffed the other.

"Because if you don't know what 'you-know-what' is, you're the sorriest excuse for a treasure hunter the world has ever seen. My four-year-old daughter knows what 'you-know-what' is." sighed the thief.

"But that 'you-know-what' you just said could be something else other than 'you-know-what'." the person sitting across from the thief said.

"Okay, you know what? You're giving me a headache, that's what. Now do you want to hear the rest of my story, or no?"

"Yeah, continue."

"Now I'm thinking, 'Oh my Goddess, I've hit the mother lode!' as I ran into the room. I was careless, but in the presence of an Arcanian artifact that's worth more than you can imagine-" the thief was suddenly interrupted.

"I dunno, I can imagine a lot." chuckled the companion.

"Enough!" the thief slammed his fists onto the table, causing their drinks to spill. "I took three or four steps and the next thing I knew the floor gave way and I was in another room with all these monsters! It's a miracle I made it back alive."

"Why would monsters be there?"

"Prolly attracted to his freaky experiments if you ask me." the thief shrugged.

"There's something flawed with your story, Jantero. How did you get past the Treasure Hunters Society guard?"

"Heh, he was sleeping when I made a break for Tekky's Tower. I don't think he'll be sleeping on the job any time soon though, he caught me running from the tower and threatened to press charges on me for cheating the Treasure Hunters Society out of its hard-earned credits." Jantero coughed, "Said I had to register an adventure before I would be allowed in the building officially."

"Don't you think that Tekky guy is pissed off at the Treasure Hunters Society making money off of sending people on adventures to his tower?"

"I doubt he even knows it's going on. Like I said, all I saw were robots and monsters. I would hate to be the one to tell him all his stuff is being taken by tourists though. He doesn't have all his screws tightened, if you get my drift."

Lars thanked the bartender and quietly left the bar with his next destination in mind. As he opened the door, the bright sunlight pierced his eyes and temporarily blinded Lars causing him to stumble into Grunk.

"See? Man can't do anything." Grunk growled to himself as he pushed Lars off.

"Yeah, yeah. Where's Izlude?" Lars dusted himself with his hand.

"I watch kid for seven minutes, man owe Grunk two credits."

Izlude approached his brother with a smile and nodded to him. Lars placed a finger on his lip and tilted his head thoughtfully to the side.

"Say, Grunk. Tell me where I can find the Treasure Hunters Society and I'll give you five credits."

"Treasure Hunters Society far, Grunk tell for ten." Grunk haggled.

"Fine," Lars said as he dug for his credits before handing the orc ten red bills. "Where is it?"

"Man needs to go down the street one block that way." Grunk pointed with a crooked, green finger.

"...And then?"

"That's it. Treasure Hunters Society there. Big building, not even man miss."

Lars sighed loudly and motioned for Izlude to follow him. The brothers from Drom began walking down the street, Lars' pace being longer and quicker than Izlude's made him struggle to keep up.

"B-Brother?" Izlude panted as he tried to keep up with his red-haired, older brother.

"Yeah?" he responded.

"Why are we going to the Treasure Hunters Society?" Izlude meekly asked.

"We're going to the Treasure Hunters Society so we can go to Tekky's Tower so we can get the first map piece." Lars answered.

"Tekky's Tower? But why do we have to go to the Treasure Hunters Society to go there? I'm...confused." Izlude stopped walking.

"Okay, let me explain." Lars brought a finger up and left his mouth open.

Lars shook his head and grabbed onto Izlude's arm, forcing him to walk along. The sun was shining brightly, and even though Lars wouldn't say it to his brother, the combination of the heat and Izlude's questions were starting to get to him.

"Never mind. There's too much. I'll explain it on the way."

Loud, slightly obnoxious orchestrated music was being played throughout the lobby of the Treasure Hunters Society. Lars raised one of his eyebrows as he gazed upon the room. A large desk with a woman sitting behind it was in the center. Hanging above the desk was a large banner showing names of what Lars could only assume were dungeons and a price in credits beneath them. Several large, coloured posters littered the walls, all of them featuring Marina blatantly in the center with the society's logo beneath her. Both Lars and Izlude approached a particularly large poster and examined it closer. It showed an image of Marina cracking her whip with a serious expression on her face.

"Well, she's the best treasure hunter in Port Tasuna so I guess that would explain this." Lars frowned. "But I never knew her to be so...vain."

"Maybe because she's the best treasure hunter the society wanted her on all of their posters? She's well-known, right...?" Izlude pondered out loud.

"Makes sense to me. People associate the society with her now, I guess." Lars fumbled in his pockets. "We'd better have enough credits to get access to Tekky's Tower."

The two slowly began to make their way towards the desk in the center of the lobby. Lars squinted up at the banner and shook his head as he discovered that Tekky's Tower wasn't listed. An older gentleman beside Lars seemed to be lost in thought. Lars took this opportunity to get some information without appearing to be from the country.

"Hey, uh, a lot of choices, huh?" Lars motioned with his head.

"What's that sonny?! I didn't hear ya!!" the old man yelled loudly, causing everyone in the lobby to look in their direction.

"Never mind!!" Lars shouted as he jumped at the man's volume.

The people in the lobby quickly shrugged off the yelling and went back to what they had been doing before. The secretary behind the desk seemed indifferent to the random outburst and was wearing an obvious fake smile, her bright-blue hair shining in the artificial light. Lars caught sight of another man more middle-aged than the one he had attempted to talk to. He was dressed fairly well in a suit and tie and didn't appear to be the adventuring type at all. Lars approached him nonetheless and attempted a conversation with him.

"So, where are you thinking of going?" Lars asked.

"Oh, I'm not sure." the man replied. "You see, if I purchase the 'Challenge the Swamps of Mirkan' they provide a lovely boat tour but they don't provide you with food. On the other hand if I purchase the 'Search for Dragon's Bones in Quwalt Caves' you have to walk, but they do give you sandwiches and a drink."

"S-Sandwiches?! What kind of an adventure is that?" Lars stammered at the ridiculousness of what the man was saying.

"Yes, you're right. I'm much better off with the boat tour." he answered and approached the desk.

Lars shook his head and started to make his way towards the desk to enquire about Tekky's Tower. Izlude made a few more glances at the posters of Marina around the room before following his brother.

CHAPTER 16

"Treasure Hunters Society membership, please." the secretary at the desk ordered, slightly annoyed.

Lars raised an eyebrow before glancing down at Izlude. He answered Lars' expression with a slight shrug.

"Treasure Hunters Society membership?" Lars asked the secretary.

She rolled her eyes before leaning back in her chair and resting her legs on top of the mahogany desk in front of her. Her light-blue, slightly torn jeans contrasted with its regal style. She shook her head and muttered something inaudible under her breath before answering.

"You can't go anywhere under the control of the Treasure Hunters Society in this region without owning a membership." she sighed.

"Well...how do we get one?" Izlude meekly asked.

"You gotta go get a membership from our president, Mr. Kragon." the blue-haired secretary yawned while twirling her hair with her index finger.

"And where would we find him?" Lars said, his patience wearing thin.

"Behind the door to your left, knock three times and say, 'I'm Mr. Kragon's servant for all eternity.' It's the password."

"What?! I'm not saying that!!" Lars roared, causing the secretary to flinch.

"Then you can't speak to the president. Now if you don't have any other business with the Treasure Hunters Society, I suggest you leave."

Lars frowned at the stubborn girl in front of him before approaching the wooden door she had mentioned. He raised his fist in order to knock before pausing and letting his arm fall to his side. Lars then paced back and forth in front of the door, silently debating whether the loss of his pride was worth it. Izlude glanced up at his brother and thought of saying the password himself, since Lars was obviously having a difficult time with the idea. But before Izlude could, Lars straightened himself out and knocked on the door three times.

"I'm Mr. Kragon's servant for all eternity." Lars muttered.

"I'm sorry! I can't hear ya! Heh, heh." came a chortle from behind the door.

"Fine." Lars shut his eyes and bellowed, "I'm Mr. Kragon's servant for all eternity!"

The door quickly swung open and Lars, blushing from embarrassment dragged Izlude inside the room with him. The older brother slammed the door behind him and took a deep breath before examining the president's office. He blinked as he saw even more memorabilia of Marina than in the lobby. Posters littered the walls and a plastic, action figure of her likeness with a miniature version of her signature leather whip dangling beside it were just the start. A large picture framed in bright-red lay on top of the massive oak desk in the center of the room. Lars slowly brought his eyes down towards the carpet, half-expecting to see Marina's smiling face but saw he was only partially correct. The carpet was a plush bright-green that matched her hair colour.

"Now this is a bit much." Lars folded his arms across his chest.

A large chair that was positioned on the opposite side of the desk slowly spun around until it revealed a small, fidgety man in his mid-thirties. His blonde hair was curly and seemed as if nothing could possibly tame it. Mr. Kragon was also dressed in a colourful, tacky suit consisting of a rainbow-striped jacket and polka-dot pants. He sat up towards the two baffled brothers and squinted in their direction. Lars and Izlude simply stared at him.

"I take back what I said, his suit is worse." Lars corrected himself.

"What do you want with the president of the Treasure Hunters Society? Heh, heh." Mr. Kragon chortled again.

"Uh, we need a membership," Lars responded following an awkward silence, "to go to Tekky's Tower."

"Oh, that's too bad. I can't give ya one, heh."

Mr. Kragon leaned back with a smug look on his face and fondly regarded his Marina action figure. He frowned and reached into a drawer to his right before retrieving a miniature duster. With a small flick of the wrist, he quickly dusted Marina off before returning the duster to the drawer.

"B-But...we were told you could give us one." Izlude said.

"Oh, 'could' yes. But will I? Nope." he grinned a large, toothy grin.

"And why not?!" Lars yelled.

"Now, now 'servant'. Let's not be rude to your master." Mr. Kragon continued his grin, "I have too many members."

"I'm not your servant! And what's two extra people?!" Lars growled, grasping the hilt of his broadsword.

Izlude tugged on Lars' shirt and shook his head furiously. Lars relaxed his grip and clenched his teeth before he let go of the hilt.

"Yes you are. You said so when you came in! Heh, heh." Mr. Kragon jabbed.

"Let's go, Izlude. This childish idiot isn't going to let us go anywhere." Lars sighed to Izlude.

"And why am I childish, slave?"

"Because you obviously have a crush on Marina, and I'm quite sure she'll never date a loser like you." Lars replied.

"Huh. Now I'm never letting you into my society." Mr. Kragon sniffed violently while frowning.

Mr. Kragon pushed a button under his desk and two security robots emerged from a single rotating wall to the left of Lars and Izlude. They grabbed a hold of Lars before he could even withdraw his broadsword.

"Let me go!!" Lars shouted, attempting to wrestle himself free.

"Take them outside." Mr. Kragon commanded. "And for your information, Marina's my fiancée."

"F-Fiancée?!" Lars and Izlude stammered in response as they were whisked out of the president's office.

Lars cursed as he was unceremoniously thrown out of the main entrance of the Treasure Hunters Society building. He scrambled to his feet and dusted himself off while the two robots whirred around and closed the door behind them violently.

"...Bro?" Izlude quietly asked, "Why would Marina want to marry someone like that...?"

"There are only two possibilities: she has poor taste in guys, or she has a clone who looks exactly like her and shares the same name." Lars answered. "Either way, let's go talk to her. Maybe she can convince that moron to let us go to Tekky's Tower."

Lars adjusted the broadsword in his belt and broke into a brisk pace with Izlude trailing behind him.

Lars and Izlude asked directions to the outskirts of town from anyone who would respond and before long they found the western exit. Upon leaving the city, the two brothers came across a large, grassy hill with what appeared to be a wooden cabin at the very top. Lars brought his arm to his forehead and wiped the sweat off. The mid-day sun seemed to be stronger outside and around the outskirts of Port Tasuna, leading Lars to believe the dome acted like a sort of filter. Lars craned his neck up, following the steep incline of the grassy hill all the way up to the cabin before groaning.

"Why does Marina have to live at the top of the tallest hill I have seen in my entire life?" he sighed.

"Maybe she likes the view...?" Izlude offered.

"Could prolly see the Goddess' kingdom from there, let alone Drom." Lars said. "Let's get started."

Lars began to trudge up the hill, occasionally leaning forwards and pressing his hands against the steep path for balance. Izlude seemed to be having a much harder time. The distance was slowly gaining between Lars and himself. Lars paused for a quick second to glance down at his younger brother before offering a hand in his direction with a smirk.

"You can do it! We're almost there." Lars nodded in encouragement.

Izlude grasped his brother's hand and allowed Lars to pull him towards his older brother. Lars looked up the path and back at Izlude before shaking his head.

"Alright, I lied. We're not even half-way there." he panted.

As the pair continued to climb the steep hill, Lars couldn't help but notice a shriekgull floating lazily in the azure sky. Shriekgulls were scavengers and were known to make a quick meal out of anything dead they could find. Its auburn feathers seemed to shimmer in the sunlight while it slowly circled the two youths from Drom. Lars motioned towards it with his head before laughing.

"Maybe that shriekgull knows something we don't." he chuckled, out of breath.

Lars grabbed a large fistful of grass with his hand and over-dramatically struggled onto the top of the hill. He lay motionless on the ground aside from his heavy panting. Izlude slowly climbed up behind him and cautiously poked Lars with his finger.

"You'll have to continue on without me," Lars groaned. "It was nice knowing you."

Izlude poked Lars a couple more times before he flailed in response.

"Leave me to rot in peace!" he winced.

Izlude simply stared at his brother until Lars eventually conceded and stood up. He stretched his arms back and blinked at the wooden structure in front of them. The cabin wasn't the largest one Lars had seen in Drom, but neither was it the smallest. A set of four stairs led up to a quaint patio with two windows and a tan, wooden door. It appeared to be well maintained from the outside, and neither Lars nor Izlude could figure out how Marina could have possibly kept up with repairs and hunting for treasure at the same time. The two brothers cautiously made their way to the door, creating loud creaks on the patio as they did so. Lars shrugged and knocked three times. After waiting for an answer for thirty seconds, Lars moved past Izlude to one of the windows before looking inside.

"She doesn't seem to be home, bro..." Izlude said. "Maybe we should come back later?"

"And climb this mountain again?! I don't think so." Lars responded harshly. "We're staying right here."

Lars folded his arms against his chest and leaned against the door. It quickly swung open from the pressure and sent Lars sprawling on his back inside the cabin

"Of course." Lars groaned.

CHAPTER 17

Izlude approached his older brother and helped him back onto his feet. He looked down at Marina's carpet and then to their leather shoes, which were covered in dirt from their recent hike.

"Bro...we should probably take off our shoes. I'm sure she'd want that..." Izlude suggested.

Lars nodded while rubbing his behind. He then kicked off his leather shoes, as did Izlude. The foyer they were in had several paintings hung on the walls and Izlude glanced at them all as he followed Lars further into the cabin. The foyer opened up into a large, combined living room and kitchen. A wood-burning stove sat next to another window overlooking the hilltop with four chairs around a small table in front of a fireplace. A fire was going strong, and several pieces of Marina's clothes seemed to be drying on a rope in front of it.

"Hey Marina!!" Lars yelled. "Are you home?!"

When no response came, he sighed and sat down on a chair. It creaked in protest as Lars shifted his weight so that he could lean on the table in front of him.

"Where could she be?" he mumbled through closed eyes.

A sudden creak from the foyer caused Lars to snap his eyes open. He stood up quickly and readjusted the chair he had been sitting on back to its original position. A click came from the foyer hall around the corner.

"Marina...? Is that you?" Izlude spoke.

"Izlude?! My Goddess, guys! I thought you were thieves!" Marina came around the corner while holstering her beam-gun. "You're lucky you said something."

"Where were you, anyways?" Lars frowned.

Marina walked over to the counter beside the wood-burning stove. She then opened a satchel on her hip before removing a handful of herbs. She placed them on the counter and crouched in front of the cupboard underneath.

"I was on the other side of the hill collecting burgalow herbs for the stew I was going to make for lunch." she answered as she took a metal pot out of the cupboard and placed it on the stove before turning to face them. "Don't tell me you've found a piece already?"

"Yeah, we have. But your moron of a fiancée won't let us get to it!" Lars shook his head.

"Fiancée?" Marina asked as she tilted her head in confusion.

"Mr. Kragon, the joker who happens to be the president of the Treasure Hunters Society." Lars looked away in disgust, "How could you marry a jerk like that?"

"Oh that bastard!" Marina growled. "Is that what he's been spreading around town now?"

She slammed her fist on the wooden table causing Lars and Izlude to jump backwards in shock. Marina closed her eyes and took a deep breath before removing her hand from the tabletop as she turned away from the brothers. Lars looked down at Izlude and met his eyes. He motioned with his head for Izlude to say something to Marina, but Izlude shook his head furiously. Lars ran his fingers through his bright-red hair before approaching her.

"He wasn't that bad, actually..." Lars said as he walked in front of Marina. "Okay, I'm sorry, but he was that bad."

"Don't apologize! I hate him! Mr. Kragon's lower than a green slime!" she shouted in response.

"Okay, okay!" Lars brought his hands with his palms facing her. "Why are you marrying him then?"

"I'm not. He just wants me to. It's a long story..." she replied softly. "Are you guys hungry?"

"A little..." Izlude answered.

"You have to ask?! Last I ate was hours ago!" Lars patted his slim stomach.

"Then I'll tell you over lunch." Marina giggled lightly.

Lars leaned slightly backwards in his chair and stretched

his arms over his head before sighing. A content smile crept across his face as he looked down at the steaming bowl of stew in front of him. He was addicted to Marina's cooking by the first bite.

"Marina, what did you put in this stew? I've never tasted anything like it!" Lars said.

"Well, the burgalow herbs help to bring out the flavour of the ingredients. It's an old trick my sister taught me..." Marina reminisced quietly.

"Um, Marina?" Izlude quickly interrupted. "What's going on with Mr. Kragon?"

"I've known that weasel since I was a little girl. He was always in my face about being his lover. He never stopped saying how I was going to love him eventually and how it was fate that brought us together. I don't really know what brought us together, but I really wish it hadn't. He used to try horribly skewed romantic things towards me as the years went on, which sadly evolved into blackmail." Marina answered.

"Blackmail?" Lars raised an eyebrow. "What could he possibly have on you?"

"It's not what he has, it's what he can take away..." Marina sighed dejectedly.

"What do you mean, Marina?" Izlude asked.

"When my sister left me, I was trying to find something to do with my life, so I joined the Treasure Hunters Society. I was a good friend of the old president's and he convinced me to join. He said that I could search for my sister with their help and that he would give me enough training to go off the tourist map. You know, real dangers and real treasure. Most transportation is controlled by the society. They either get a percentage cut of all of their generated income, or they own it entirely. Joining seemed like a great idea at the time, but by the time I found out who the president's son was..."

"So, Mr. Kragon got the position when his dad left. What's he threatening you with?" Lars asked.

"He's told me numerous times that if I didn't return his love for me, that he would cut me off from the Treasure

Hunters Society entirely. That would mean searching for my sister would become impossible. I wouldn't be able to go on any adventures legally anymore, and Cyrus would most likely become grounded." Marina sighed.

"Adventuring illegal? You can't place laws on adventuring! What kind of adventure is it when everything has to be set in stone?!" Lars yelled.

"This isn't a world where that's possible!" Marina yelled back. "Everything is different out here compared to Drom!"

A knock on the door broke the yelling. Marina sighed while placing her spoon down on the table before standing up. She paused for a moment in the foyer hall and turned to face Lars.

"I'm sorry I lost my temper, Lars." she said, "This whole thing just has me a little on edge."

With that said, she walked out of Lars and Izlude's sight towards the door. Lars shrugged and continued to eat his stew. He placed a hearty spoonful into his mouth but was interrupted by a scream from the front door before he could so much as chew. His eyes darted to Izlude's and the two of them quickly rose from their seats. Lars withdrew his broadsword and charged after Marina with Izlude close behind. They found the door askew and Marina a few meters outside in a heated conversation with Mr. Kragon. He appeared to have arrived in some sort of enclosed hovercraft, which was directly behind him. Lars examined it from a distance and agreed with his thoughts that it appeared similar to the one he and Kilik had hijacked before.

"My love! We're only moments away from being together forever and ever!" Mr. Kragon dreamily stated. "The priest is waiting in the Goddess' Chapel for us!"

"I'm not marrying you! Get that through your head, Mr. Kragon!" Marina protested. "I don't love you!"

"Is this guy bothering you?" Lars asked her as he slowly approached them.

"Oh, it's you. You're still not joining my society. Stay out of business that isn't yours." Mr. Kragon snorted, turning back to Marina. "Now why won't you marry me? I'll even give you breakfast in bed every night!"

"Don't you mean morning?" Lars raised an eyebrow while muttering.

"I can't marry you, because..." Marina trailed off and looked at Lars.

"Because?" Mr. Kragon asked.

"Because I'm engaged to Lars!" Marina yelled happily as she threw herself into his arms.

"You're what?!" Lars, Izlude, and Mr. Kragon shouted in unified astonishment.

"You're going to have to play along for this to work, Lars." Marina whispered harshly in his ear.

"Uh...yeah. We're getting married! We really...er...love each other." Lars stammered.

Strong gusts of wind were the only thing that could be heard on the hilltop after Lars' statement. The awkward silence was thicker than Marina's stew. Mr. Kragon made a cough and blinked at Marina.

"So you can't marry me!" Marina cheerfully said. "I'm sorry we weren't able to be together, but you'll find someone else who you deserve, I'm sure of it."

"Yeah, like the Chief of Drom." Lars muttered under his breath.

Mr. Kragon's expression quickly turned to one of determination. He suddenly brought his fingers to his lips and let out a piercing whistle. Lars grabbed his ears and winced until Mr. Kragon's whistle finished.

"What the heck was that for?!" Lars snapped.

"Marina, my soon-to-be wife! Your future husband will save you from this slave and then we will be married tonight!" Mr. Kragon cheered.

"What are you talking about, you-" Lars began.

A very sharp pain in the side of his neck cut him off. Lars staggered backwards as he felt a sudden dizziness overtake him. His vision began to blur until he eventually collapsed onto one knee.

"Lars!!" he heard Marina yell from what seemed like miles away.

Lars brought his hand to the side of his neck and pulled

118

out the tranquillizer dart, which seemed to dance hypnotically in his palm. Lars cast his gaze hazily up towards Marina. He extended a weak arm to her as he saw Mr. Kragon grab her arm and drag her towards the hovercraft. Lars' arm dropped heavily to his side before he fell onto his second knee. A man clothed in a dark cloak briskly walked past Lars and nodded to him. He slung the dart gun over his shoulder and entered the hovercraft along with Mr. Kragon and Marina.

Lars eventually lost control of his muscles and collapsed onto the grassy hill beside Izlude who apparently had also been hit with a dart and had succumbed earlier to its toxins. Lars struggled to get up in order to give chase to Mr. Kragon's hovercraft that was now speeding away, but his energy was completely gone. His eyes forced themselves shut and Lars slipped away to the realm of unconsciousness.

Izlude heard explosions and a trio of voices yelling. They seemed familiar to him but at the same time foreign. He saw flames erupting among the rubble that littered the room and upon inspecting it he discovered that a great battle must have occurred shortly before. He spotted three shapes blurred by the shadows and waves of heat that were being emitted from the flames surrounding him. Two appeared to be weakened with the third standing steady, yet all three were breathing heavily. The smallest of the three was determined by Izlude to be female and was on her knees in front of a glowing sphere.

"We had a deal, did we not?!" roared the third. "The Arcanian for your child! This is what happens when you steal what is the rightful property of the Lucarian army and incur its wrath!"

"What makes you think you can take our new-born son in exchange for a human life that wasn't yours to begin with? Answer me, general!!" yelled the other man, obviously infuriated. "Sapphire's and my own flesh and blood! You're

119

nothing but a sick bastard, and you'll rot in the depths of hell!"

"Relics, please...he still has our child. I...I don't think I could live with myself if anything bad happened to him!" the female pleaded, her voice in pain.

"Stay strong, Sapphire. We'll get through this!" the second man assured her. "He needs a mother. You'll be fine after we get you back to the Steel Falcon, I promise! Just keep that wound from bleeding as much as you can."

Izlude tried to approach them, but the scalding flames blocked his path. He watched as the man who was referred to as Relics ignited his beam saber.

"After fighting all twenty of my men, you still have fight left in you?" mused the Lucarian general. "Very well, Relics. Fight for your child! Know that the only way to release him from his spherical prison is to defeat me!"

The general withdrew his beam saber and both Relics and he began to fight. They were broken up several times by falling debris but re-engaged soon after it impacted the ground. Izlude could tell that Relics was exhausted but he didn't seem to want to give up his struggle. The duel eventually brought the two men to the edge of what seemed to be a bottomless pit. Relics quickly glanced down at the gaping hole behind him before looking up at the general.

"You've met your end, Relics! Drop your beam saber and I will make your death quick!" the general smugly stated.

"That's what you think!" Relics shouted as he whipped out his grappling hook and shot the end at his opponent, piercing his stomach.

The general roared in pain and anger. Relics took this brief moment of opportunity to pull hard on the firing mechanism of his grappling hook. The general fell over the edge and plummeted into the darkness, but not before stabbing his beam saber through Relics' chest on his way past him. Relics stood in shock for a few moments. He then staggered towards Sapphire and fell on his knees in front of her. The sphere that was in front of her dissipated, revealing a small, strangely silent baby.

"Damn it..." Relics coughed blood, "I'm sorry, love...but it looks like I won't be there to raise our son...I was...careless."

"Relics! No...I love you! You'll be alright! Tell me you'll be alright!" Sapphire cried, "He needs you! I need you..."

"I wouldn't have...made a good father anyways..." Relics forced himself to speak, "Raise him well, Sapphire...remember...you'll always be my everything..."

With that said, Relics collapsed to the ground and lay motionless. Sapphire cried out his name and sobbed for what seemed to Izlude to be a very long time. She carefully picked her child up off the ground and cradled him gently in her arms. The small child now had tears streaming his face and was crying incessantly.

"You will be just as strong as your father was...I know you will be." Sapphire soothingly spoke to her baby, "I...I know I won't be there to raise you myself...even though I wish I could be...but your mother is hurt too much...It even hurts her to breathe...but please remember my voice and always know that I loved you, that your father loved you...Oh, Goddess...please watch over my son, follow him where he goes and protect him...There, there...Everything is going to be fine...I'll try to stay with you until Daron or our other friends come...Everything will be alright."

CHAPTER 18

Izlude felt disoriented as Lars kicked him awake from his dreams. He groaned and sat up slowly.

"C'mon! We've got to go after Marina!" Lars shouted. "We'll make that Kragon pay!"

Izlude rubbed his eyes with the back of his hand sleepily before nodding in response. He allowed himself to be picked up to his feet by Lars. The sun was very close to setting and neither Izlude nor Lars was sure just how long they had been unconscious. What was for certain though was the fact that travelling to Port Tasuna the way they had arrived would take longer than they had time for. Lars brought his hand to the top of his head and scratched it while looking at the domed city.

"We'll never make it in time, bro..." Izlude sighed in defeat.

"We just need to get a little creative is all!" Lars happily announced as he spotted a shack beside Marina's cabin.

He motioned for Izlude to follow him and approached the door. Lars extended his hand, grasped the handle and pushed it inside. Various pieces of what Marina probably referred to as "junk" littered a counter near the back wall. Lars placed a foot inside the shack causing the boards beneath him to creak in protest.

"Well there goes that plan." Lars coughed. "Could've sworn Marina would've kept something interesting back here, like a bazooka or something. Any ideas, Izlude?"

"Why don't we use this sled?" Izlude suggested.

"Hate to break it to you, but there's no snow. So unless it starts snowing really quick, we'll fall flat on our faces at the start." Lars shook his head, "However..."

"Are you sure this is going to work, bro...?" Izlude asked

his brother with uncertainty.

Lars had discovered a very slippery oil in one of the barrels in the shack. He had rubbed it against the metallic runners on the bottom of the sled that Izlude had found and placed the sled in front of Marina's cabin. Izlude was now sitting on the front half of the sled with his brother standing behind it ready to give it a large push.

"Of course it is! All of my ideas have worked so far, haven't they?" Lars grinned.

"Somewhat..." Izlude muttered.

"Hang on tight, Izlude!" Lars shouted. "Because here we go!!"

Lars shoved the sled with all of his might and quickly hopped on behind his younger brother once they reached the edge of the hill. The oil Lars had slopped onto the runners seemed to do its assigned task well, perhaps too well. The moment Lars had landed behind Izlude, the sled rocketed downwards at breakneck speed towards Port Tasuna.

"I think we're going too fast! Slow it down, bro!" Izlude squinted through the blasts of wind.

"I can't!" Lars shouted. "But look on the bright side! We might just make it!"

Lars grinned largely as he began to enjoy the ride down. To him this was a far better way to travel than the method they arrived by. Izlude's pointing ahead and shouting derailed Lars' train of thought.

"We're going to run over those shriekgulls!" Izlude yelled as he brought his arms up to cover his eyes.

The shriekgulls had finally discovered something worthwhile. They were happily eating away at the carrion of some old monster when Lars and Izlude flew like a beam shot towards them. The shriekgulls screeched and hastily flew off in a flurry of feathers as the brothers from Drom passed.

"I-I don't think we hit any..." Izlude stated, turning his head to look at Lars.

Lars coughed, causing a few feathers to exit his mouth. Because of the velocity at which they were travelling, the feathers were immediately left behind. Izlude looked at the disgruntled expression on his brother's face and held back a laugh. Lars shook his head and pointed directly in front of them with his finger.

"We're almost at the entrance to Port Tasuna!" Lars suddenly cheered.

"B-But it looks like there's someone there!" Izlude said. "And he doesn't look friendly..."

"Eh?" Lars squinted in the distance.

The guard had been standing next to the western entrance of Port Tasuna for many hours, ordered by Mr. Kragon to ensure that people by the name of Lars and Izlude didn't try to disrupt his wedding and the citywide reception afterwards. It had now been four hours since the leader of the Treasure Hunters Society gave him the order and the guard was starting to doubt that they would ever show up. He sighed dejectedly and shook his head. Mr. Kragon had threatened to force the mayor to send the guard into the unemployment office if he failed and the guard believed him. He knew that Mr. Kragon held a lot of say in almost everything that happened in Port Tasuna because of how much he stimulated the economy.

"Although, those kids didn't seem like they were particularly evil when they passed through." the guard muttered to himself.

He yawned and stretched his arms up to the sky before cracking his neck to the side. He opened his eyes and spotted a dust cloud zooming down Burgalow Hill directly towards him and the western entrance.

"...the hell?" he said to no one in particular as he tried to determine what was causing the anomaly.

The guard brought his right arm up and behind his shoulder. He grasped his beam saber in its scabbard that was strung against his back. After withdrawing it, he braced himself into a combative stance. Monsters had been appearing more often lately and he didn't want to take any chances with the dust cloud that was storming its way towards him. He remained steadfast preparing himself for the inevitable battle he knew was coming. The gate guard grinned as he daydreamed of various honours and medals that would be bestowed upon him for defending the defenceless citizens within the walls of Port Tasuna. Each time he replayed his dream in his mind the creature he battled grew fiercer and fiercer.

He was quickly cut off from his daydreams when the dust cloud reached a closer proximity. The guard's eyes widened as he thrust his hand out and screamed for Lars and Izlude to stop immediately.

"Just get out of the way!" Lars yelled back. "I would've stopped a long time ago if I could!"

"Y-You're not allowed to enter the city b-by order of...of..." the guard stammered.

Frozen in fear, the gate guard could do nothing as Lars, Izlude, and the sled crashed directly into him. Lars and Izlude were both tossed forwards where they landed on the grass along with several pieces of wooden shrapnel from the now-destroyed sled. Lars stood up and patted his arms. He frowned as he glanced down at the remains of the sled and shook his head.

"C'mon, man! You broke the sled!" Lars shouted at the guard flat on the ground. "You'd better apologize to Marina later, or you'll catch holy hell!"

"I'll slay you...terrible creature...protect everyone...hero..." the guard muttered in a dazed state.

"Terrible creature?" Lars asked.

"Your fangs'll be...crushed and minced..." he continued.

"That made even less sense." Lars rolled his eyes.

Lars Nokuten bent at the waist and grabbed the hilt of the guard's beam saber. The crash had sent it to the ground and the resulting impact had caused the laser to dissipate back into the hilt. Lars slid the green button up slightly as he had seen done before and the blade immediately shot out of its metallic base. He nodded in silent approval and tossed it to Izlude after sliding the button back down. Izlude caught it awkwardly and stared at the weapon.

"B-Bro? Is it safe?" Izlude asked his brother nervously. "I don't even know how to use it!"

"You'll get the hang of it, don't worry." Lars answered as he spotted the guard's scabbard strapped to his back. "And besides, I can't let you keep being unarmed. I can't protect you all of the time. Hey, mind if I take this?"

"Key to the city...rewards..." the guard kept muttering.

"I'll take that as a yes." Lars shook his head as he unhooked the straps off the guard's back.

Lars placed the scabbard on his own back taking only a few moments to readjust the straps to match his own specifics. He withdrew his broadsword from his belt loop and slid it inside the small scabbard. It seemed to be a perfect fit. While it was designed to hold a beam saber hilt, which was only eight inches in length, it had an open bottom, which allowed Lars' blade to slide through. He swung his arms around for a short while, adapting to the shift in weight before nodding to Izlude.

"Alright! Let's crash this wedding!" Lars cheered.

He pumped his fist and the two brothers from Drom made a dash towards the western gate. Lars paused for a moment and looked over his shoulder at the gate guard.

"Hey, you know where Mr. Kragon and Marina Jayd are supposed to get married?" he asked him.

When no response came, Lars shrugged and they continued on their way.

Marina awoke. She was bound and gagged on top of a plush, royal-red carpet. She struggled with her bonds for a short while before giving up. Marina sighed through the cloth gag that was wrapped tightly around her head and looked up. The brass symbol of the Goddess' Church of Port Tasuna hung in front of a large stained glass window, the reflecting colours dancing in every direction. The effects of the tranquillizer dart administered to she while inside the hovercraft were only starting to wear off and she still felt severely disoriented. The closing of a door caused her to flinch and snap her head in its direction.

"You're awake, my love! This is good!" Mr. Kragon beamed.

All Marina could do was create muffled yells and shouts aimed at Mr. Kragon while he slowly approached her from the door he had entered. He adjusted his tacky suit and cleared his throat before approaching his bride-to-be.

"Now, now," he comforted, "we'll be married soon! And then we can be together forever and ever! Yup!"

A sound of disgust emerged from behind the gag. Mr. Kragon seemed to ignore it and turned to face another door in the church. He tapped his foot a couple of times before glancing at a watch on his wrist.

"What could be keeping the priest? Doesn't he know we don't have all day? We need to go on our honeymoon!" Mr. Kragon frowned.

Marina struggled with her chains violently before eventually conceding. She closed her eyes and silently prayed for a miracle. She hoped that Lars would come and rescue her from the situation she was in, even though Marina didn't realistically expect him to. After all, this was a problem she knew she should have sorted out a long time ago.

CHAPTER 19

All of Port Tasuna was bustling and Lars and Izlude had to force their way past people several times. It seemed as if the whole town was a massive pre-wedding party. Izlude was glad that Lars was beside him and made sure that he wasn't being left behind but at the same time, he wanted to pause and catch more than glimpses of what was occurring around him. Izlude turned his head to the side and saw a burly man of small stature chugging a bottle of red liquid. He appeared to be severely intoxicated but was ignoring this fact. Izlude was not sure if this was because he wanted to or just didn't realize it.

"This is useless." Lars muttered.

As the two brothers were walking, Lars attempted to ask where he could find Marina and Mr. Kragon but to no avail. The town was more interested in the party aspect than the wedding itself. Lars spotted a disturbance in the crowd and slowly approached it with Izlude. There they saw a youth not much younger than Lars arguing with three guards clad in full riot gear consisting of a thick vest, leg and shin covers, and a helmet and visor that completely blocked the face from view of the public.

"I just want to get my brother! He said he was going to the Goddess' Church to see Marina in her wedding dress and he hasn't been back!" the youth shouted at the city guards.

"He wouldn't have been allowed in even if he had. He must have been denied entrance and gone home. This is the third time we've caught you loitering around the church. Once more and you're being tossed into the city jail." the captain of the guards tersely stated as he adjusted his helmet and visor.

That said, the guards quickly turned around and marched away. The youth cursed at them before folding his arms and quickly walking in the opposite direction. He grumbled loudly and was not paying attention to where he was walking. This was made obvious by his walking straight into Lars.

"Ah...sorry there. I'm just really distracted." the youth

sighed.

"Hey, hold up." Lars grabbed his shoulder as he tried to pass by. "You said your brother's at the Goddess' Church?"

"Yeah, the idiot wouldn't take no for an answer. He's had a crush on Marina for a while even though he's only seventeen. I kept telling him that Marina's far out of his league, but no, he had to go and try to see her." the youth explained.

"We'll get him for you. Where do we find the Goddess' Church?" Lars nodded.

"You look serious!" the youth exclaimed while looking at the broadsword on Lars' back. "Maybe it's best I don't know what you're up to...If you find my brother, tell him to meet me in the square. I'll be waiting there for him."

The youth relayed the directions to the church to Lars and Izlude before bowing in thanks and running into the crowds. Lars watched as he disappeared from view and then proceeded to follow the route to the church.

"Hang on, Marina. I'm coming." Lars whispered inaudibly to himself.

A small crowd of a dozen or so people were protesting greatly outside the gates of the Goddess' Church. Standing stalwart in front of them were several guards dressed in riot gear. Neither Lars nor Izlude were sure of which guards had reprimanded the youth because of the extensive gear they had on, but they knew they were among them. The two brothers from Drom were positioned behind a large bush twenty feet from the small, disgruntled crowd.

"But I've known Marina since she was a little girl! Surely you'll let me bear witness to her marriage!" a portly woman with greying hair exclaimed.

"For the last time, both Marina and Mr. Kragon have declared that they don't want a single soul to see them until afterwards. You'll have plenty of time to mingle and show your emotions later during the citywide reception." responded a guard.

"I'm telling you all that's false!" a familiar voice shouted to everyone. "She mentioned nothing of a wedding while she was on the sky ship I work on! And even if she wanted to get married, do you honestly think she wouldn't want anyone there for it?"

Lars eyes tried to dart around the various people before finding the source of the voice. Hikari struggled greatly as two guards violently grabbed his arms and dragged him past the bush that Lars and Izlude were hiding in and then out of sight of the crowd. They threw Hikari to the ground and withdrew their beam-guns. Hikari scrambled back and raised his hands towards the guards.

"N-Now hold on! Take it easy!" Hikari said nervously.

"If I hear another word of you trying to spread rumours, I will personally kick your teeth in and slice your tongue off! Do you hear me?!" the guard on the left roared.

"Loud and clear." Lars answered from directly behind them.

Lars placed his hand behind his back and withdrew his broadsword. The guards, surprised at the voice behind them, turned around as Lars had expected. With a quick slash of his broadsword he sliced their beam-guns in two. Several sparks flew from each half of the guards' weapons before exploding into puffs of smoke on the concrete. Lars kept his broadsword pointed towards the guards as he cycled back and forth between them.

"You know, you guys shouldn't be so rough with people. You never know when someone like me will get the upper hand!" Lars chuckled.

Izlude struggled with his beam saber trying desperately to ignite it. He grimaced as he pushed the small, green button upwards. The beam saber's blade finally stretched up and formed a point three feet from its hilt. Izlude nodded to his brother and pointed the beam saber at one of the guards allowing Lars to focus on one.

"You're making a big mistake!" the guard shouted.

"I doubt they'll hear you and even if they did, they're not allowed to leave their post." Lars shook his head.

"It's probably best just to listen to him." Hikari grinned as he stood up and dusted himself off.

"Hikari, how's it going?" Lars smiled to the bartender of the Sky Princess.

"Pretty good or at least it was. I was on my way over to the Heaven's Fist to grab myself a pint of beer when I found out that Marina was apparently getting married. I never thought she would be one to get married, I always considered her a free spirit. You know what I mean?" Hikari replied. "Something just doesn't feel right..."

"She doesn't want to get married, Hikari..." Izlude said to him.

"What?" Hikari frowned.

"Well...Lars and I were there when Mr. Kragon abducted her..." Izlude explained.

"I knew it!" Hikari yelled. "Did you bastards know about this?"

The guards glanced at each other before shaking their heads. Hikari was apparently unconvinced since he moved around them until he was standing directly beside Lars. He then removed one of the guards' helmets before he balled his hand up into a tight fist and slammed it into the guard's chin. The guard staggered backwards. He grimaced and roared with rage while bringing his own fist up and charging towards Hikari. Lars brought his broadsword up causing the tip to force the guard to stop his attack. The guard blinked as the broadsword tip dug slightly into his throat. Lars shook his head and the guard slowly backed up a few steps. He rubbed his chin vigorously where Hikari had struck him before glaring at the bartender.

"Hey, Lars?" Hikari shook his fist to get rid of the slight pain from the impact. "Let's get rid of these guys and we'll talk a little more."

"Sounds like a plan!" Lars said, "Turn around."

The guard in front of Lars complied however the one in front of Izlude hesitated slightly. He appeared to be eyeing the way Izlude's blade shook. Lars spotted this and turned to face Izlude. He saw that his younger brother's hands were shaking severely. Whether this was out of nervousness or from simply being scared of the brute in front of him, Lars was not sure. He placed his hand directly on top of Izlude's and nodded to him before pointing his broadsword at the guard in front of him. Izlude relaxed and nodded in silent thanks and struggled slightly as he pulled the green button down. The beam saber withdrew into the hilt in his hands. The guard looked at Lars' expression and eventually complied as his partner had. Hikari glanced at the first guard before removing the second guard's helmet.

"Sorry!" Lars happily said to the guard in front of him.

Lars brought down the hilt of his broadsword sharply on top of the guard's exposed head. The guard shuddered slightly before collapsing into a heap onto the concrete in front of the trio. Lars and Hikari looked expectantly at Izlude and he gulped.

"S-Sorry..." Izlude repeated.

Izlude closed his eyes and swung the hilt of his beam saber towards the other guard's head as hard as he could. A small thud was heard and the guard brought his hands up to his skull and rubbed it sharply.

"Ow!! Why the hell did you-" the guard began.

Lars quickly interrupted him by slamming his own hilt into the guard's head, properly finishing the job. The guard collapsed in a similar way next to his companion.

"Let's get these guards behind the bushes before someone sees them." Hikari suggested.

After several minutes of dragging on the part of Hikari, Lars, and Izlude, the unconscious guards were safely concealed behind the bushes that Lars and Izlude had been behind only moments before. Lars clapped the dirt from his hands and turned to face Hikari.

"So Marina doesn't want to marry Mr. Kragon?" Hikari asked Lars.

"I'm pretty sure she'd marry a swamp goblin before Mr. Kragon." Lars replied. "The guy's a complete jerk."

132

"I've never met Mr. Kragon to be honest, but I'll take your word for it." Hikari nodded, "Then what are we going to do? The Goddess' Church is locked up pretty tight. Mr. Kragon's got security all over the place."

"No matter what it takes I'm stopping it. We just need a way to get inside..." Lars thought out loud.

"Bro...? What if we do what we did to get on board the Sky Princess?" Izlude said softly.

"You mean...?" Lars answered, "I like it!"

Lars adjusted the guard's helmet and frowned. He was clad in the guards' riot gear but found it to be very uncomfortable. Even though it fit Lars like a glove, he was surprised at the weight of it all and felt a slight amount of pity towards anyone who had to wear it.

Izlude was worse off. The gear fit him very poorly and even after adjusting the vest to the smallest possible, he was still swimming in it. Lars was convinced, however, that Izlude could pass as the second guard. Granted, he was shorter than the other guards positioned in front of the Goddess' Church.

"I'll try and find another way in and join you guys inside the church walls." Hikari said. "I'm not that good in combat but I'll try my best."

"Alright," Lars' voice was muffled by his riot helmet, "then we'll find a back entrance and stop all of this."

"You be careful, Lars." Hikari nodded to him.

"Yeah, you too. Don't go doing something stupid like trying to climb over these fifteen-foot concrete walls." Lars chuckled, tapping his broadsword against the one nearest him.

He sheathed his broadsword behind his back and they split up. Hikari quickly made his way around the outer church walls and disappeared from sight. Izlude pushed his riot vest up towards his chest fiddling frantically with it. He was very doubtful that his current stature would pass and that Lars and himself would actually slip past the guards' eyes. They didn't even know the guards' names like Lars and Kilik had known when sneaking onto the Sky Princess. Izlude nervously bit his lower lip as they approached the group of guards. One particular guard cast a scrutinizing glance towards Izlude. Fortunately, an older man with grey hair storming towards the front gates broke his gaze.

"Now see here! I demand to be allowed entrance into the Goddess' Church! Don't try and stop me! You young whippersnappers don't know the first thing of respecting your elders!" the older man bellowed, "Why back in my day..."

"Sir, it doesn't matter how old you are. You're not allowed through," replied a guard.

Lars was thankful for this interruption since they were easily able to slip through then. Lars motioned noiselessly with his head for Izlude to follow him around the church to the back and the brothers silently moved around the corner. Various small shrubs decorated the western wall of the Goddess' Church and they appeared to be very well maintained. Heavy footfalls from the backside of the church broke Lars' assessment of the foliage and he instinctively reached for his broadsword. If it were a patrol, he would definitely have a fight on his hands.

The footfalls didn't seem to be making any progress towards their direction or any other direction for that matter. Lars Nokuten, slightly taken aback, glanced down at Izlude and nodded before the duo quietly made their way towards the strange noise. Lars frowned and held up his palm towards Izlude. Izlude froze in his tracks and Lars pressed himself against the wall. He slowly inched himself towards the corner. Unfortunately, as he did so he happened to step on a dry branch. It snapped loudly and Lars flinched. The heavy footfalls stopped. Lars took a deep breath before sprinting around the corner with his broadsword brandished in front of him.

"Whoa!!" Lars and a youth in front of him both shouted in shock.

Lars' broadsword remained a few inches from the stranger's face. The youth took a couple of careful steps backwards before bowing low.

"F-Forgive me! I know you've told me not to loiter but I can't help it!" he apologized with his eyes shut tight still facing the ground. "P-Please don't hurt me!"

"Y'know, you look awfully familiar." Lars commented as he sheathed his broadsword behind him.

"I think this is that person's brother..." Izlude suggested from behind Lars' back.

"Oh yeah! I kind of forgot about that." he frowned from behind his visor, "Will you stand up straight already? We're not going to hurt you and it's embarrassing!"

"W-What?"

"Um...Lars? It might help if we took off those guards' uniforms..." Izlude commented.

Lars shrugged and removed his helmet and riot gear. Izlude did the same and was immediately grateful to be without them.

"Your brother sent us to find you. He...uh...wants you to meet him in the square." Lars relayed the request.

"H-He did? You're not Mr. Kragon's guards?" the youth asked.

"Do you really think they'd let Izlude here into riot gear?" Lars chuckled slightly. "Sorry about the scare, I heard footsteps and thought you were one of them."

"Oh..." the youth sheepishly stuck his hands in his pockets, "I was trying to jump high enough to look in that window up there to see if I could catch a sight of Marina."

He pointed as he spoke to a large window several meters above the ground and well out of even Lars' sight. Lars quickly glanced around for a back entrance but realized that other than the out-of-reach window and a dusty, old shack in the corner of the yard there was nothing else.

"I guess we'll have to force our way through the front door, Izlude. Just leave the fighting to me, alright? I don't want you to get hurt. Our parents would be rolling in their graves if they knew what we were up to-" Lars was interrupted by the youth before he could finish.

"You really want to see her too, huh?"

"Yeah, something like that." Lars answered with a shrug. "Why?"

"Well...there's another way inside if you think you're at least strong enough to take on those guards in the front."

"Eh?" Lars raised an eyebrow.

"There is a secret passageway that was made a long time ago as an escape route from inside the church. I'm positive you could still use it to get inside!" the youth nodded.

"...Why didn't you just try that instead of the whole window thing?" Izlude asked the youth.

"That's the catch. I tried to earlier but had to run from the slimes and all of the other monsters that have made homes there."

"It's never easy huh, Izlude?" Lars grinned, "Take us to the entrance! We'll show those monsters a good time."

Lars whipped his broadsword in a small circle by rotating his wrist before sliding it into its sheath. Izlude turned to face his brother incredulously. He couldn't help but think that sooner or later his older brother's luck would run out. Izlude was positive he never wanted to see anything bad happen to Lars and quickly tugged on his arm.

"What about Hikari?" Izlude blurted out.

"He can find his own way. The longer we wait, the more of a chance that Marina's going to be married to that creep!" Lars charged towards the small shack with the youth.

CHAPTER 20

The youth struggled as he moved an awkwardly placed small cast iron stove off of a hidden trapdoor. Lars tilted his head to the side slightly while contemplating why something less obvious wasn't placed in its stead. Having finished his task, the seventeen-year-old dusted his hands off before standing up and looking at Lars and Izlude.

"It's just through there," he explained, "but it's a complete maze inside. You might get lost."

"We're never lost! We just go sightseeing." Lars grinned.

They lifted the trapdoor and the brothers from Drom leapt inside, plunging into the darkness below. Their feet landed on the hard floor causing Lars to stick his hand on the ground before standing up straight. He looked up at the youth's face and nodded.

"Alright. You'd better head to the square and meet your brother. We'll take care of it from here!"

"Good luck!" the youth saluted and closed the trapdoor.

Lars paused for a moment as he heard the cast iron stove dragged back on top of the trapdoor. Izlude took his beam saber out of his pocket and ignited it. An eerie, green glow penetrated the darkness, revealing a small foyer. The walls dripped with water and the smell of pungent mould filled their nostrils. A pathway beckoned for Lars and Izlude to travel further and before Izlude could take a step, he felt Lars' hand on his shoulder.

"If there's anything here, you'd better get ready for a fight or run away! Lars Nokuten, Captain of the Mercenaries is psyched and ready for a brawl!" Lars shouted.

"Bro...now everything knows we're in here..." Izlude muttered in defeat.

"Exactly. Nothing will jump out at us now. They'll all be waiting to fight us or running away in terror!"

"...But what if they decide to ambush us?" Izlude pointed out.

"Er...uh..." Lars scratched the back of his head, "Didn't

think of that."

Izlude cringed dramatically at his brother's words and they slowly walked towards the north. Lars withdrew his broadsword in preparation for the onslaught of monsters that could occur at any moment. He noticed Izlude trying to hide his fear from him, but decided against bringing it up. Lars would never admit to feeling an increasing sense of nervousness at the submerged dungeon that lay before him. Their steps echoed endlessly in all directions.

"Stay close, Izlude. It'd be impossible to find anyone here if they got lost." Lars cautioned.

"...But how do we know which way to go?" Izlude asked. "We don't have a map..."

Lars shrugged and looked around the four-way intersection they had come across. He turned his head and squinted into each of the three other directions before looking down at Izlude.

"Well, here's where we have to start making choices."

The sudden noise of a flurry of footsteps blasted towards Lars and Izlude. Lars quickly brandished his broadsword in front of him and tilted his head in each direction to determine the location of its focal point. Izlude nervously did the same, the bright-green aura quivering around them as he shook.

"Beside us?" Lars questioned no one in particular.

He turned to the left just in time to be face to face with Hikari. Both Hikari and Lars screamed loudly at the sudden encounter. Their yells roared throughout the secret passageway much like Lars' announcement of his arrival had.

"Thank Goddess! Lars, you've got to help me! A monster is after me!" Hikari explained, out of breath.

"Monster, eh?" Lars asked curiously while taking a step and motioning for him to follow. "What kind?"

"I... I don't know, Lars. It sprung at me while I was trying to find you. I heard your shouting earlier and got a little lost. Then all of a sudden I was being chased by this creature! I didn't exactly stop to take a look."

Lars, Hikari and Izlude carefully travelled the path that Hikari had come charging from. Lars paused after a few dozen steps down the hallway before stopping.

"Izlude, pass me your beam saber for a bit, would ya?"

"S-Sure, bro..." Izlude nervously responded.

While his sentiments towards the beam saber had been anything but positive earlier, with the mention of monsters he was glad to be holding onto a weapon. He was reluctant to get rid of it so easily, but he knew his brother would give it back to him when he was finished so he relinquished his grasp on it. Lars took the beam saber from Izlude's hand and shined it in front of him. He squinted into the darkness while using the beam saber as a lamp. All that could be heard was Hikari's heavy breathing until Lars spotted a small collection of water on the cold, stone floor.

"Don't worry, Hikari! I'll save you from that puddle!" Lars shouted dramatically.

Lars and Izlude looked at each other before sharing a hearty laugh. Hikari folded his arms and shook his head. He couldn't fathom why his attacker had given up their chase.

Perhaps it recognized it was about to be outnumbered? he thought.

"C-C'mon, Hikari!" Lars gasped for breath. "Let's head back to the intersection and work on saving Marina."

Hikari nodded and the trio began walking back the way they came. A low gurgling noise caused Lars to suddenly pause in mid-step. He frowned and glanced over his shoulder. After trying to find its source, he gave up. Lars silently shrugged to himself. A small shimmering caused him to look at the floor.

"Do you guys remember seeing more than one puddle on the way here?" Lars commented on his observations.

"No, why?" Hikari replied.

"No reason..." Lars frowned and turned his back to the puddle.

They began to walk again, their shoes creating echoes that bounced along the waterlogged walls. The gurgling noise occurred again. This time it was Izlude's turn to look over his shoulder. What he saw sent a surge of adrenaline through his body. Izlude threw his body against Lars' and sent him crashing into Hikari. The slime's blue, crystallized arm missed piercing Lars' back and instead continued on its path, creating a large gash on Izlude's forearm. Izlude grimaced and pulled his arm towards his chest.

"What's the big idea, Izlude?!" Lars shouted. "What the hell?!"

Lars leapt off the ground and tossed Izlude's beam saber back to him. The slime withdrew its weaponized body part and it became a viscous shape again. The glow from the beam saber shot through the slime making it look eerie. Hikari began to back up slowly while facing the attacker.

"Lars! It was the puddle! It was biding its time to attack!" Hikari shouted loudly.

Lars nodded to Hikari before charging towards the monster. He brought his broadsword down and cleaved the slime neatly in two. Both halves of the slime slunk to the ground and sat as two small puddles on the stone.

"I told you to get ready for a fight or run away!" Lars taunted. "Now look at you!"

Lars chuckled and turned around to check on Izlude and his injury. He took a few steps forward before both Hikari and Izlude shouted at Lars to look behind him. He frowned and quickly did so. Instead of seeing a single slime preparing for an attack there were now two slowly approaching Lars, their upper halves each taking on a rough, humanoid shape.

"What the...?" he proclaimed, "Izlude! I'm gonna need your help! Get the one on the left!"

"W-What?" Izlude stammered, clutching his arm.

"Slicing it in half isn't going to work! It'll just help it to divide!" Hikari shouted.

"Then what do you suggest?!" Lars grunted as one of the slime's arms solidified and struck his broadsword.

"I'm a bartender, not a treasure hunter! Give me time to think!" Hikari answered. "Hold on! I'll be right back!"

"Where are you going?!" Lars yelled at Hikari as he passed him.

The second slime attempted a vicious lunge at Hikari but missed latching onto his ankles by mere centimeters. The sailor looked over his shoulder nervously and continued on his way. Lars managed to force the slime attacking him away from his broadsword but had to repress the idea of countering with an attack of his own. It frustrated him playing a defensive battle and having to only rely on parrying to keep himself alive.

Meanwhile, the second slime had advanced to Izlude and was attacking him as well. Izlude struggled greatly against its attacks. Lars wasn't sure how long his younger brother would last and silently hoped that Hikari would be back sooner rather than later. Lars knew that his stamina would see him through for quite a while longer, but Izlude had never swung a sword before. Lars was always getting into "sword fights" with Kilik when they were younger and Izlude wasn't in the picture yet. They always used wooden sticks or broom handles as weapons. Their mothers scolded them often but Daron Nokuten had been supportive of his son.

"He's a boy, Natalia. Do you recall the old adage? Boys will be boys?" Daron had said so many years ago.

"Stop defending him from punishment, Daron! If you let him go unpunished you are only teaching him that he may act however he wishes to!" Natalia, his mother, had responded.

On that particular night, Lars and Kilik had managed to shatter the chief's window during a particularly aggressive moment of combat. Daron had finally returned to the village after his journey on the Steel Falcon. He had brought Lars a gift but the chief had confiscated it, much to the frustration of the six-year-old. Lars was never told what the gift had been and his father only said that it had been a memento of his travels with Sapphire and her crew.

Lars was shaken from his memories by a particularly strong attack. He threw a kick forward that he regretted the moment he started it. His leather shoe embedded itself inside the slime and a cool, stinging sensation started to envelope his ankle. Lars tried to keep his balance on one foot but the wet stone floor beneath him caused him to slip. He then watched in horror as the slime began to pull itself further up his body.

141

"Bro!" Izlude cried out desperately.

He was struggling with the other slime's arm and his own beam saber was slowly approaching his face. Tears were streaming down his cheeks from his previous wound and Lars' predicament, which Izlude knew he could do nothing about. Rapid footfalls echoed down the hall.

"Hold on for a few more seconds!" Hikari yelled.

He ran towards the brothers with a makeshift, wooden torch in hand and swiped the flames at the slime in front of Izlude. It screeched in agony and was immediately burned to a crisp. The second slime, seeing its twin disintegrated, latched onto Lars harder.

"Damn it, Hikari! Pull me out before you fry it!" Lars shouted while being dragged further in.

Izlude extinguished his beam saber and threw it in his pocket. He grabbed onto one of Lars' arms and desperately struggled to pull him out. Unfortunately for their predicament, all he could do was slow down Lars' consumption by the slime. Hikari ran to grab Lars' arm with his free hand but was also unable to do any good with only one arm.

"Put the torch down and use both of your arms!"

"But, Lars! If I were to do that... the water might put it out!" Hikari strained.

"Stick it in my mouth then!" Lars commanded.

"W-What?" Hikari blinked.

Hikari turned the wooden torch on its side and placed the three-foot pole in Lars' mouth so that the flames were to the side of his body. He quickly grasped his ally's leather glove and pulled with all of his might. Slowly, Lars began to be pulled out of the cool, burning liquid.

"Good! I'm almost out!" Lars mumbled from behind the torch.

The slime relinquished its grasp on Lars and slunk to the ground before attempting to crawl away. Lars scampered onto his feet and pulled the torch from his mouth. He casually walked up to the slime and disintegrated it with the flames.

"I hope I never get that feeling again." Lars shivered.

He brushed off some of the bluish liquid that had solidified on his pant legs but was interrupted by an angered roar from somewhere deep in the passageways. Lars stood at attention and brandished his broadsword at the darkness in front of him and then behind him.

"I think we've upset something," he said while looking around with the torch.

CHAPTER 21

Izlude looked down at the fresh bandage on his arm. He was fortunate that Hikari had brought along a medical kit. He frowned and pulled his shirtsleeve down on top of it. It'd be best not to think of it. Izlude, Lars, and Hikari had been wandering the secret passageways for a short while and hadn't managed to find anything other than dead ends.

"Another dead end?" Lars slapped his hand to his forehead, "You've got to be kidding me!"

"Maybe we missed something?" Hikari suggested.

"Like what?" Lars sighed as he slashed his broadsword at the stone wall in front of him.

The resulting clang reverberated throughout the waterlogged hallways. Izlude flinched in surprise and Hikari frowned. Lars looked at the two of them and shrugged.

"...Do that again, Lars."

"What?" Lars looked at Hikari. "Like this?"

Lars swung his broadsword against the stone wall a second time and the same clang echoed down the halls. Hikari approached the stone wall and knocked on it with his fist. He then proceeded to feel the individual stones that were embedded in the wall. Lars folded his arms across his chest before looking at Izlude. The two brothers exchanged looks of confusion and intrigue.

"Uh, what're you doing, Hikari?" Lars stared.

"That sound. It was similar in pitch to metal colliding with metal." Hikari responded as he held the torch up against the wall.

"Metal on metal, huh? Are you saying these stones are metallic?" he asked the bartender.

"Not exactly. I think there might actually be..." Hikari twisted a particular stone and pushed the hidden door inwards, "a door."

"Whoever made these passages are starting to quickly make their way up my list of impressiveness." Lars said as he entered the next room.

"List of impressiveness...?" Izlude asked his brother.

"Yeah, Nak's not on it."

Izlude and Lars let out a small chortle. Izlude always looked forward to these moments that he had with his brother. He knew that no matter how difficult or dangerous the situation they were in, Lars would always be there for him with words of encouragement or at the very least, a distraction. Izlude followed behind Lars and was quickly followed by Hikari.

"Who's this Nak guy?" Hikari questioned with confusion.

"Oh, that's right. You don't know about Nak, do you?" Lars smiled. "Nak's a good friend of ours-"

"Lars! There's movement!" Hikari suddenly shouted while pointing inside the room.

Lars snapped his attention to the direction of the point in just enough time to see four slimes slip beneath another door to the north. He cautiously entered the next room with his broadsword ready to slice anything that moved. After glancing around for any other signs of life, he sheathed his broadsword behind his back.

"Why did they run, Lars...?" Izlude asked.

"Psh, they're probably scared of us. Can't blame them."

"No, Lars. They're planning something. It doesn't feel right." Hikari speculated.

The room they had just entered was covered in dust. Various racks of weaponry littered the floor. Lars walked towards one particular rack and poked a great axe. The metallic head was severely warped and the wooden pole it rested on was already splintering.

"This passageway must be really old." he said.

Hikari nodded and approached the opposite door. He grabbed the handle and slowly tried to turn it. It wouldn't budge. The bartender bent at his waist and looked inside the keyhole. He squinted in an attempt to penetrate the darkness but to no avail.

"It's locked, Lars. We're going to need a key." Hikari said.

"It's either in this room, or it's been lost. We didn't see a key when we were searching the outer passageways."

"I still don't see why we can't just slice the door in two with Izlude's beam saber." Lars said as he sat down on a small, metallic chest.

"Watch where you're sitting! This is definitely not a place fitting!" a loud voice boomed through the room.

Lars jumped up from the chest and grasped his broadsword. Izlude ignited his beam saber and shakily held it in front of him. Hikari grabbed a slightly warped dagger from a nearby weapon rack and backed himself up against the wall next to the door.

"Who said that?!" Lars demanded.

"You seem to be surprised by how I greet, your answer lays simply at your feet." the voice replied.

"Eh?" Lars glanced down at his feet, "There's nothing here but dust and a chest...Hikari! Don't breathe! The dust is talking to us!"

"The dust is incorrect, my friend. Your perception fails you in the end!" the voice chuckled.

"So it's the chest." Hikari said while lowering his dagger. "It's magic seems to be very potent, be careful, Lars."

"Magic? So it's Arcanian. We might have found a piece of the map!" Lars proclaimed as he tapped the metallic box with his foot. "But how do we open it?"

"You will not simply open me! The items inside do not come free!" the box explained, "Three riddles I have, some quite easy. Beware the harder ones will make you queasy. A guess each you shall receive, but be wary, I aim to deceive."

"Riddles? I was never good at those." Lars sighed.

"There doesn't seem to be anything bad about losing, let's give it a go. We're stumped here at the moment regardless." Hikari suggested.

"I'll give it my best, bro..." Izlude nodded.

"My first riddle, I offer thee. Doesn't it fill you with glee?" the chest hopped slightly from the ground, "You get many of me, but never enough. After the last one, your life soon will snuff. You may have one of me but one day a year. When the last one is gone, your life shall disappear."

"Not going to lie, I have no idea." Lars coughed.

146

"You get many of me, but never enough..." Hikari mumbled to himself, "One day a year...when the last one is gone..."

"A birthday...?" Izlude asked the chest.

There was silence. Hikari looked at Izlude with an expression of surprise. Izlude shuffled awkwardly, silently praying that he was right. After a few seconds, he spoke.

"I'm sorry..." he muttered.

"Don't be, Izlude. That would have been my guess, but it appears it's something else..." Hikari replied.

"A birthday is right! Your goal is closer in sight!" the chest suddenly stated.

Lars pumped his fist and nodded happily towards Izlude. Izlude, filled with relief, let himself sink to the floor. He sat with his legs sticking out and sighed. He was glad that he hadn't lowered their chances of success.

"One down, two to go. That was an easy riddle to let you know. I'm afraid that it only gets worse. You must answer this before you line your purse." the chest continued.

"Purse?" Lars raised his eyebrows.

"Only a bit of poetic license, nothing I say has to make sense." countered the chest.

"Alright, alright!" Lars replied while holding the palms of his hands towards the chest. "What's the next one?"

"I have many tongues but cannot taste. By me, most things are turned to waste. I crack and snap, yet stay whole. I may take the largest toll. I assisted all of the first men and I will pay them back again. Around me, people snuggle and sleep yet run when I am released from my keep. I jump around and leap and bound. The cold man wishes I he had found." it rhythmically stated.

"If it were me, I'd say alcohol." Hikari laughed.

"C'mon, Hikari! Marina's waiting for us to save her!" Lars said. "Take it more seriously."

"What? It works if you force it." Hikari shrugged, "I've seen all sorts of reactions to it as a bartender on the Sky Princess."

"Alcohol is incorrect, it seems your brain is that of an

insect. Your chances have fallen to two more, you are losing opportunities to score!" the chest said while doing a small hop.

"Ugh, this is starting to give me a headache. My head feels like its on fire!" Lars groaned.

"Here," Hikari rummaged through his medical kit, "take these pills. It should help."

Hikari tossed Lars a bottle. He caught it and popped the lid. He carefully picked out two red pills from inside and threw them in his mouth. Lars swallowed them dry and nodded to Hikari.

"The answer is indeed fire, most impressed am I! You solved it fairly quickly and on your second try! I may have underestimated you, keep on fighting through!" the chest cheerfully announced.

"Huh. It must have thought I was saying the answer when I said my head was on fire." Lars blinked in surprise, "Well, two down and one more to go."

"As I was going to St. Ives, I met a man who had seven wives. Each wife had seven sacks, each sack had seven cats each cat had seven kits. Kits, cats, sacks and wives, how many were going to St. Ives?" the chest spoke with its lid.

Silence filled the room. Lars stared at the chest incredulously, hoping that this riddle was a joke. He frowned as he desperately tried to do the math in his head. Izlude gave up shortly before Lars did, but not by much. Hikari seemed to still be lost in thought.

"Oh, come on! That's ridiculous! There can't be over two hundred things going to St. Ives!" Lars shouted.

"No, you're wrong, Lars. I've got it." Hikari nodded.

"Well? What's the answer? Five thousand and two?" Lars shook his head.

"Nope." Hikari grinned, "It's one."

"How do you figure? It just asked us how many things were going to St. Ives. That includes all of the cats, sacks, and wives." Lars commented.

"That's just in there to confuse us. Think about it, 'As I was going to St. Ives,' just him, no one else. It's never suggested that the man and his wives are actually going there." Hikari explained. "The answer is one."

"Your answer strikes true! It seems that with riddles you are not someone new. However, I must apologize for you were far too slow. Your timing was definitely against the flow! Unfortunately you will be forced to regret where you have strode. I must now bid adieu and simply explode." the chest admitted.

"What?!" Lars exclaimed and jumped back with his arms covering his face.

"Ten, nine, eight..." the chest began.

Hikari grabbed Lars and Izlude before pulling them towards the door they had entered from. It quickly slammed shut. Hikari desperately tried to pry the door open with the dagger he had grabbed earlier, but the blade snapped inside.

"Seven, six, five..."

"Lars! It's locked!" Hikari grunted while pushing, "Help me out!"

"How far do you think it'll reach?" Lars replied while straining against the door.

"Four, three, two..."

Lars shoved Izlude, Hikari, and himself into a corner near the door and they huddled themselves together with their eyes shut tight in preparation for the explosion. Lars placed his hand on the back of Izlude's head and attempted to shield him.

"One!"

The trio's faces and bodies tensed up drastically. They waited for the loud noise they expected to hear just before the explosion, but it did not come. Lars slowly relaxed his face and opened his eyes. They met Hikari's and Izlude's. Lars frowned at the two of them before slowly straightening himself up. The chest immediately roared into a loud, boisterous laugh.

"Hah! I couldn't resist doing that little jest! You should have seen your faces when you thought you failed my test! But my time is indeed up, that was no lie. At least I had enjoyment, and you gave it a try. Without further ado, I offer up my treasure. You certainly earned it, with no other amount of measure. When you see my contents, you will offer up a tune. Look me up later next time, see you soon!" the chest melodically stated.

The chest stuck a long, red tongue out at Lars before cackling and swinging its lid wide open. Lars slid his broadsword out of its scabbard and poked the Arcanian chest. He looked behind his shoulder at Hikari and saw him shrug. Lars brought his attention back to the chest and knelt down beside it. He replaced his broadsword to where it had been moments before and cautiously stuck his hand inside the now open chest. He frowned as his hand touched two cold, metal objects. Lars grasped onto them and pulled them out.

"Well there's our key..." Lars said, "but what's this necklace?"

The two objects Lars had taken from the chest were an ornamental key and a necklace: a round, azure sphere of an unknown material suspended inside a metallic cage. While there was hardly any light in the room the three of them were in, whatever meager amounts that caught it reflected brilliantly.

"It seems to be safe," Lars speculated, "but we did find it inside that...weird chest."

"It's almost mesmerizing." Hikari straightened himself up, "It must be worth something."

Lars nodded and held the necklace in front of Izlude. Izlude blinked and took a step backwards. He shook his head violently.

"I-I might lose it! Or...or break it!" Izlude stammered.

"Then you lose it." Lars grinned, "Go on take it. I trust you."

Izlude nodded slowly and took the necklace from Lars' open palm. He swallowed and placed it around his neck. The azure orb felt surprisingly warm and Izlude pondered if this was normal. Meanwhile, Lars stood in front of the door with the key in his hand, looking extremely confident while Hikari helped himself to another dagger.

"Now, no more delays! We've got to save Marina!" he

shouted.

"Uh, Lars?" Hikari said. "It's this door here. We came in that one."

Lars looked at the door in front him. He tilted his head to the side before blinking and turning around.

CHAPTER 22

The dank dungeon was very demoralizing for Izlude. He found it hard to fight against recurring dark thoughts of hopelessness. They had only spent just under an hour travelling the secret passages under the church, yet it seemed like an eternity. Izlude wondered whether he, Lars, and Hikari would ever see daylight again. Lars still maintained his determination and boldly marched onwards. The door had led the three of them to a very long hallway. They had spent the past five minutes walking this hallway and it appeared to simply continue on forever due to a large collection of mist slowly approaching them. It obscured even Hikari's keen eyesight but he and Izlude were the only ones beginning to feel concerned about its presence.

"That fog's starting to get a little close, Lars." Hikari reminded him.

"It's kind of foreboding, bro..." Izlude threw his two cents in.

"It's just a bit of mist. I'm more worried about us starving to death before we find the end of this hallway!" Lars shook his head and trudged onwards.

Hikari suddenly shot his hand out, grabbed Lars by his shirt and pulled him back. Lars flailed as he tried to maintain his balance. He eventually caught it and glared at the bartender.

"What's the big idea?" Lars said.

"I didn't meant to scare you, Lars, but-" Hikari began.

"You startled me. I wasn't scared." Lars interrupted.

"Regardless, look!" Hikari pointed and hissed.

Lars frowned and followed the direction that Hikari's finger was pointing. He spotted movement and squinted to see through the mist. A light-blue glow emanated from it for a short second. It was definitely a slime.

"Is it trying to ambush us?" Lars whispered.

"No, I don't think so..." Hikari pondered out loud. "It looks like it's trying to go somewhere."

"Trying to go somewhere...?" Izlude asked. "But it's a monster...where could it be going?"

"Exactly where we're going!" Lars nodded.

"What?!" Hikari and Izlude responded immediately.

"Keep a low profile so it doesn't see you." Lars ordered. "C'mon!"

"It's a slime, Lars." Hikari blinked, "It doesn't have eyes. And besides! Why do you want to follow it? We should be thankful it didn't notice us."

"Something tells me that if we follow it, we'll find the entrance to the church." Lars replied. "What choice do we have? Unless you plan on walking through one of these walls somehow."

"I don't like this. Something doesn't feel right..." Hikari stated.

Lars ignored his comment and continued on his path towards the mist, stopping a few feet from it. The fog lapped at the trio's ankles as if trying to draw them further in. Lars squatted and tried to clear it with his flat palm. He was only mildly successful as he managed to barely expose the ground they were walking on.

"Lars, we should hold hands." Hikari suggested.

"Eh?" Lars answered, taken aback.

"In case we trip or a slime grabs one of us." he explained.

"You're right. Good idea!" Lars nodded to Hikari.

Lars, Izlude, and Hikari all grasped hands. Lars slowly began leading the way into the dense mist, followed by Hikari. As Izlude was being guided into the mist, he took a deep breath before releasing it. He hadn't said it to his older brother, but he agreed with Hikari's feelings. Izlude was as sure as Hikari that something was wrong but he saw how Lars dismissed Hikari and assumed that he would be as well.

The mist quickly progressed from Lars' ankles to well over his head. There were a couple of times, as he slowly walked forwards, that he felt the sharp sting of the uneven stone wall on either side of him. He found it nearly impossible to keep his path straight with no bearing ahead of them. If Hikari didn't have a tight grip on Lars' right hand, he wouldn't have even been aware of his existence. The torch that Hikari had used to burn the slime had long since extinguished. The dense mist was very humid and had attacked the flames viciously.

"Keep your ears open, Lars. At least we've still got our hearing." Hikari's voice echoed.

Before Lars could respond, he felt his stomach suddenly soar up to his chest. He had attempted to place his foot on the floor but something was lacking: the floor itself. He tipped forwards and yelled as his second foot came with him. Hikari was caught unawares. He stumbled forwards and had the unfortunate luck of slipping on a patch of water on the stone floor. He yelled in unison with Lars and the combination of their weight yanked Izlude down the pit with them. Wind streamed by their faces and their screams echoed loudly throughout the passages.

Mr. Kragon frowned from his position beside the bound and gagged Marina. He scratched the back of his head and looked at both the priest and his bride to be. The priest looked just as confused as he did, and Marina had stopped her struggling temporarily.

"Huh. Did any of you hear that too?" Mr. Kragon sniffed.

"It sounded like some sort of war cry or scream of utter terror." the priest responded.

"Yup. Maybe both?"

Marina groaned and wished she could slap her hand against her forehead. The fact she was about to be married to the most despicable man she had ever known was easily trumped by the fact she was captured by someone as stupid as he.

"My wife is being impatient! We need to be married!" Mr. Kragon turned to Marina, "Don't worry, dear! We'll be married soon! Yup!"

Marina moved her head back and squinted her eyes in

disgust. She turned to face the priest and silently pleaded for him to let her go. The priest caught her eyes but was immediately interrupted by Mr. Kragon shoving money at him.

"This'll help you to forget that interruption! Yup, yup! Go on with the wedding!" Mr. Kragon smiled.

Lars felt cold water rush up his body as he plunged into a small pool of water along with Izlude and Hikari. His feet touched the bottom and he used it to launch himself to the surface. Lars broke the water's edge and managed to drag himself onto a landing. He coughed up some of the water he had swallowed before flipping onto his back. Hikari and Izlude burst out of the stagnant pool shortly afterwards. They also pulled themselves onto the landing and collapsed.

"I thought the whole point of holding hands was so that this didn't happen." Lars groaned.

"At least we're still alive." Hikari replied while on his stomach. "Although I don't know where we are now."

"Did we ever know where we were...?" Izlude said as he spat out some water.

"Touché." Hikari coughed.

Lars placed his hand on the floor and shakily stood up. He leaned against a nearby wall and waited for Izlude and Hikari to do the same. He turned his head slightly and looked down the new path before them, thankful his view wasn't blocked by any mist. He could see a fairly large room looming ahead. Several concrete pillars could also be seen, only a handful still supporting the roof.

"Only one way to go." Lars lazily motioned with his arm to the room ahead of them.

Hikari stood up and together with Lars helped Izlude to his feet. Izlude reached into his pocket and withdrew the beam saber he had been given by his older brother. He caressed it with his eyes before igniting it. The familiar green laser shot out of the hilt and created the blade. It flickered slightly, but otherwise appeared to be functioning normally.

Izlude brought his attention back to Lars and Hikari. They were already making their way towards the large room that lay in front of them. Izlude quickly slid the beam saber back into his pocket and ran to catch up. Upon reaching the entrance, Lars glanced up at the ceiling. It rested several dozens of feet above the three youths. Its only source of support was the pillars and the crumbling walls that circled beneath it. The room itself was large and circular with two other passageways that linked up with it. An archaic crest lay directly in the middle, tarnished and forgotten. Lars raised an eyebrow and walked to the middle of the room. He looked down both passageways before looking at Hikari and Izlude.

"Well now which way?" Lars shrugged. "Want to flip a credit?"

The sound of splashing caused Lars and Hikari to withdraw their broadsword and rusty dagger respectively. Izlude, seeing this, fumbled for his beam saber and ignited it. Hikari dragged Izlude towards Lars and the three of them each looked down a different passageway.

"Nothing over here!" Hikari whispered harshly.

"I don't see anything, bro..." Izlude murmured.

Movement caught Lars' eye and he braced himself. It seemed like the whole hallway they had just walked down was slowly moving towards them. He wiped his eyes with the back of his hand and squinted. Several blue slimes were oozing their way towards the trio. Izlude tugged on Lars' shirt and pointed down his own passageway. Lars glanced quickly in its direction and saw the same thing occurring there.

"Lars, we're trapped!" Hikari shouted, his passageway was also producing slimes.

"Damn it! Back up to the wall!" Lars commanded.

The three of them slowly back-peddled to the wall behind them and stood their ground. After a few moments' wait, the slimes began to emerge. Instead of attacking immediately, however, they slowly began to gather together on top of the crest.

"What are they doing?" Lars asked Hikari. "Are they scared of us or something?"

"I'm not sure..." Hikari replied.

A solitary slime perked up and stood tall and thin amongst the other slimes. Lars grabbed the hilt of his broadsword and remained at the ready should the slime decide to charge. But, to Lars' confusion, no other action on the slime's behalf followed. A second slime perked up and did the same as the one before it. It paused for a second before merging itself with the first, causing it to grow substantially in size.

"Oh my Goddess..." Hikari muttered with his eyes wide.

"What?" Lars and Izlude responded

"It's a queen slime! They're making a queen slime!" Hikari said.

"A what?" Lars blinked.

"When a slime feels that it can't absorb another creature safely, it'll group en masse and attack their prey as a large, single monster!" Hikari explained.

Slime after slime rapidly began to perk up and add itself to the growing mass of slimes before them. Lars cautiously moved towards the western passageway, sliding his back along the wall as he did so. He quickly discovered that a menagerie of slimes blocked the passageway. Upon spotting Lars, they crystallized themselves, creating a temporary wall. The surprised Lars Nokuten debated silently for a short second whether to approach the slimes or not but quickly decided against it. He edged his way back to Hikari and Izlude. He shook his head when their eyes turned to him.

"W-What're we going to do?" Izlude stammered as the queen slime continued to grow.

"Don't get too close," Hikari cautioned Izlude, "it'll try and pull you in like it did to Lars."

"The way it's growing, we don't have much choice!" Lars gritted his teeth and unsheathed his broadsword.

It shimmered slightly as it reflected the massive slime before them. The last slime added itself to the blue mixture and the queen slime was complete. It paused only for a moment before changing its upper half into a humanoid shape like the smaller versions were prone to do. Lars tilted his head up to look at its "head" and gulped. It occupied the entire height of the room and was only a few feet from the cracked roof.

"I don't suppose you've got an extra-large torch on you, Hikari?" Lars chuckled nervously.

"We're going to need another plan, Lars!" the bartender said.

"Then until we think of one..." Lars grinned with a sudden rush of courage, "we'll give it all we've got!"

Lars hopped into a battle stance brandishing the Arcanian broadsword in front of him with both hands. Hikari nodded to him and retrieved the rusty dagger from his bag. Hikari stood beside Lars and nodded to him. Izlude fumbled for his beam saber and ignited it before cautiously approaching his brother and Hikari. Three spiked "arms" suddenly erupted from the upper torso of the humanoid shape and darted straight towards the trio.

CHAPTER 23

Lars shouted a battle cry as he clashed his broadsword against the crystallized arm interrupting its path towards his chest and deflected it into the wall behind him. It remained stuck in the wall briefly before de-crystallizing itself and returning to the center mass. A loud crash roared through the room as a large piece of the wall landed on the floor in front of the two brothers and the bartender from the Sky Princess. Lars looked from the wall to the queen slime thoughtfully.

Izlude was struggling with the crystallized arm that was assaulting him continuously. He didn't have the strength to force the arm away from him. All he could manage to do was repel it slightly.

Hikari wasn't much better off. The rusty dagger he had grabbed from the weapon room that held the Arcanian chest didn't leave any room for error. The small blade barely managed to keep the arm from piercing his flesh. Lars ran up to Izlude while bringing his broadsword over his head. He waited for the crystallized arm to launch another strike at his younger brother before delivering one of his own. He brought his broadsword down violently and sliced the queen slime's crystal weapon in half. It fell to the floor with a crash and shattered into several pieces. The remaining half quickly retreated to the queen slime while the shattered pieces on the ground left their crystal state and began to ooze slowly towards it. The queen shifted position slightly before sprouting another two blue, slimy arms. Izlude staggered backwards and stared at the massive slime in front of him.

"I-It's a losing battle, bro..." Izlude panted as Lars sliced the arm that was attacking Hikari. "It keeps making more!"

"Hikari, why is it only making three arms?" Lars asked, taking this brief pause in attacks to catch his breath.

"Slimes aren't the smartest of monsters," Hikari explained breathlessly, "it sees three targets, so it's using three arms."

"That's what I'm counting on!" Lars grunted as he swung his broadsword at a crystallized arm.

159

This time, Lars sent the arm directly into a nearby, intact pillar. With the amount of force it had behind it from suddenly attacking Lars, it easily sliced straight through the pillar. Lars grabbed both Izlude and Hikari and pulled them a few feet away. The queen slime, as Lars had expected, returned its crystal arm to its preceding state and withdrew it from where it was buried. The room began to vibrate slightly until the top half of the old, concrete pillar snapped off from the roof and came crashing down on top of the queen slime.

"Yes!" Lars pumped his fist excitedly.

The queen slime paused for a moment before retracting its arms and humanoid body and slowly enveloped the fallen support structure. Having done that, much to Lars, Izlude's and Hikari's dismay, it created another humanoid upper half and produced another three arms. Lars wiped the sweat forming on his brow with the back of his hand.

"Hikari, any ideas?" Lars asked.

"This room doesn't look stable," Hikari said, "the roof is really only held up by those stone pillars. We can't keep knocking them down or we'll be crushed!"

"Yeah, there're only four left..." Lars said to himself before grinning.

Lars broke into a sprint towards one of the four remaining pillars on the opposite side of the room. He kept careful watch of the queen slime's movements in case any attack was launched at him. Lars blinked as he suddenly saw all three arms fly towards him. He threw himself forwards and landed on his stomach. The crystallized arms shot past him allowing Lars to stumble onto his feet and continue his path.

"Lars, you psycho!!" Hikari shouted at him.

"W-What's he doing, Hikari?" Izlude said.

"He's going to try and cave the whole room in on top of it!" Hikari replied.

Izlude bit his lower lip and silently prayed that his brother would be all right. Meanwhile, Lars had found the first pillar. He stood in front of it and waved his free hand at the queen slime. It sent a single arm towards Lars' head. Lars Nokuten waited until nearly the last second before ducking, causing the weapon to crash into the pillar. The pillar began to tilt towards the wall beside it before crashing against it. Lars grinned roguishly and began to run to the second remaining pillar. The queen slime's other two arms had relinquished their assault on Lars and returned to attacking Hikari and Izlude.

"Whatever you're going to do, do it fast, Lars!" Hikari groaned as he struggled against endless attacks.

Lars ran behind the second pillar, making sure that the slime knew where he was. He sheathed his broadsword and folded his arms against his chest. He listened carefully for the sound of cracking concrete and when it caught his ears, he dove to the ground. He quickly scrambled onto his feet, just in time to see the tip of the queen slime's arm embedded through the pillar where his back had been only moments before.

"That's two!" Lars cheered and ran for the next.

"I...I thought that you said crashing the roof was a bad idea..." Izlude muttered to Hikari. "What will happen to us?"

"It's the only plan we've got!" Hikari struggled against his attacker. "I just hope Lars has thought this out well enough!"

As the third pillar crashed on top of the queen slime, Lars had a small burst of adrenaline. He only had one pillar left. Lars ran to the front of the last one similar to how he had done before. He waited for the queen slime's spiked arm to aim for his head and dove to the side moments before it would have connected. Lars heard the deafening crunch while he fell with a sense of satisfaction. It was short-lived, however, as he realized he was diving directly towards another arm. The queen slime had been prepared, or was simply lucky. Fortunately for Lars it was not crystallized, but he was immediately wrapped up and bound by the arm. Lars struggled to break free of its grasp, but the tepid ooze that had half of his body contained seemed to have a slight paralysing effect. He desperately tried to grab onto his broadsword he had sheathed earlier but was unable to. Loud, rumbling noises erupted from all around the circular room. Dust and debris fell from the roof as it began to fall apart. Lars frantically looked around for Hikari and Izlude, but they were nowhere to be seen. The queen slime slowly raised him up ten feet off the ground.

"I'm not going down without a fight!" Lars roared at the queen slime as he felt himself being pulled towards it.

A flash of green suddenly flew in front of Lars and sliced the queen slime's arm from the center body. Lars dropped rapidly with a yell. He landed painfully on his feet and stumbled forwards. Izlude's beam saber landed with a clash behind Lars, causing him to turn his head. Hikari and Izlude were standing there. The bartender picked up the beam saber and nodded to Lars.

"First time I've ever thrown a beam saber." Hikari coughed, "You okay?"

"No time!" Lars shouted. "This place is gonna collapse!"

Lars ran past Hikari and Izlude, grabbing onto the backs of their shirts as he did so. He dragged the two of them for a short while before they began to run on their own. A large section of roof crashed where they had just been and sent shrapnel flying in all directions. Lars unsheathed his Arcanian broadsword as he charged towards the western passageway and the crystallized slime wall. He swung his metallic blade against the crystal slimes but only managed to chip a few pieces off. It was a lot denser than the queen slime's arms and stood up against Lars' attacks much better. Hikari gave Izlude his beam saber back and the two of them began trying to chip at the wall. The rumbling was getting louder and louder. The trio knew they were running out of time. Lars caught a reflection of movement and turned his eyes slightly to the left to examine it. The three queen slime arms were directly behind them, fully crystallized.

"Hey, Hikari..." Lars whispered.

"I know. I see them too." Hikari interrupted.

"Good. When I say now," Lars continued, "we'll dive out of the way."

Hikari and Izlude nodded slightly and stopped chipping at the wall. Lars watched the reflection, his body tensed and prepared. He was used to the queen slime's timing, but he was worried for Izlude.

I can't think about that now, just keep an eye on it, Lars. he thought to himself.

The queen slime rapidly shot its three arms straight at them.

"Now!" Lars shouted over the chaos behind them.

Hikari, Izlude, and Lars hit the ground at almost the same time. The queen slime's arms crashed through the crystallized slime wall, effectively shattering it and opening up the passageway. The crystallized arms shattered themselves as well from the subsequent vibrations from the impact. This time, Hikari was up first. He pulled Lars and Izlude back on their feet and the three of them sprinted down the newly opened passageway.

"Are we in the clear?!" Lars loudly asked Hikari.

"Better safe than sorry!" Hikari responded. "Keep on running!"

A sudden explosion of noise erupted from the circular room that contained the queen slime. It violently shook the walls and floor of the passageway that Lars, Hikari, and Izlude were travelling. The amplified force of the impact launched the three of them five feet in the air until they landed in a crumpled heap much further up the passageway.

"Heh...gotcha!" Lars chuckled softly before collapsing on the ground.

"These noises are starting to make me nervous, yup." Mr. Kragon glared at the priest in front of him, "Are we havin' an earthquake?"

The priest's garments were very ruffled and his priestly headpiece was skewed on his head. The rumblings had occurred very suddenly and very violently. Mr. Kragon had managed to grab a hold of the small altar in front of him after shoving the priest aside. Marina, being already on the ground,

163

remained unaffected by the vibrations.

"You need to groom yourself better if you're gonna be marryin' me and my new wife here!" Mr. Kragon sniffed, "Look at ya! Your hair is messed up and your clothes look funny!"

It's the same for you, Marina thought to herself, eyeing Mr. Kragon's tacky multi-coloured suit and wild hair.

Mr. Kragon pointed for the priest to change his garments and the elderly man slowly shuffled his way towards the priest's quarters behind the altar.

"You'll look so pretty as my wife! Yup, yup!" Mr. Kragon smiled to Marina again.

CHAPTER 24

Lars slowly opened his eyes. He coughed as he inhaled some of the debris left over from the collapsed room. He tilted his head up and saw that the passageway had also collapsed a dozen feet from where they had ended up. Izlude and Hikari had landed around Lars, but lay still. He groggily stood himself up and walked up to Izlude. Lars prodded his younger brother with his boot.

"Hey Izlude, you okay?" Lars said.

"Ugh...yeah, bro..." Izlude groaned.

"What about you, Hikari?"

Hikari didn't respond. Lars frowned and approached the bartender from the Sky Princess. He tapped him with his boot like he did to Izlude, but there was no reaction.

"Hikari!" Lars shouted. "C'mon, man!"

"Y'know..." Hikari suddenly mumbled, "I dunno whether it's a good thing or a bad thing that I met you."

"Geez, Hikari! Thanks a lot!" Lars shouted while kicking him. "I thought you'd died!"

Hikari chuckled and let himself be helped up by Lars. He then ran his fingers through his hair and walked towards the large debris blocking their way. Hikari grabbed a small rock from the ground and tossed it at the impassable wall in front of them.

"We can't go back," Hikari stated, "there's no way we're getting through that."

"Then we'll go forward." Lars replied, "Marina's still waiting for us."

Hikari nodded in response. They turned around and continued down the passageway. Izlude lagged behind slightly, but kept up as best he could. He was still shaken by the encounter with the queen slime and was worried about whatever was next. Izlude let out a small cough and hurried his pace to catch up with Hikari and Lars. The passageway snaked left and right before eventually coming to an end. A severely warped, wooden ladder climbed a wall and eventually reached a trapdoor in the ceiling.

"Is it safe?" Hikari asked Lars. "Doesn't look like it'll hold much weight."

"Izlude!" Lars said, "You're the lightest. Climb on up and see how it holds."

"M-Me?!" Izlude stuttered as he backed up slowly.

"Don't worry!" Lars comforted. "We'll catch you if it doesn't."

Izlude swallowed his saliva before nodding in response. He cautiously approached the ladder as if it was ready to strike at him at any moment. Izlude gently placed a foot on the bottom rung and closed his eyes tightly as he placed more weight on it. To Izlude's surprise, it held without complaining too much. He looked behind him at Lars and Hikari and smiled slightly before slowly ascending the warped ladder towards the trapdoor.

The priest of the Goddess' Church of Port Tasuna grumbled to himself after closing the door to the altar behind him. He was tired of having to deal with Mr. Kragon and amusing him with what he considered to be the worst facade of a marriage he had ever seen. If Mr. Kragon didn't own the church and have him on his payroll, he would have had him thrown out and banned him from visiting any church in the entire continent.

He sighed and walked towards the other side of the room. The floor creaked as he traversed an ornamental rug. The priest paused for a moment to think about what would happen to him if he used the secret passages beneath the church to escape. He knew of the existence of the trapdoor beneath the rug but he was also aware that the passageways hadn't been used in centuries and that he wasn't as young as he used to be. The priest sighed and continued on his path to the opposite side of the room. There he glanced into a mirror adjusted himself for a few minutes and then began to walk back to the door he had entered.

Izlude struggled with the trapdoor. The latch was rusted and was not responding in the least to Izlude's efforts. Lars was growing impatient. He couldn't believe that they had gone to all this trouble to be stopped by something as trivial as this.

"Why can't he just slice through it with his beam saber again?" Lars shrugged to Hikari.

Hikari shrugged back and the two of them looked up at Izlude. Izlude glanced at his older brother and they nodded to each other. Izlude secured himself to the ladder and ignited his beam saber. He sliced the rusted latch off and the trapdoor swung down, leaving only fabric covering the hole. Izlude frowned at the strange sight and looked down at Lars and Hikari for some sort of guidance. They had none to offer. They were just as confused as he was. There was sudden movement on the fabric followed by a shadow over top of it. The shadow eventually enveloped the entire area of the material before a moderately large object came crashing through the hole with it leaving Izlude clinging to the side of the ladder and plummeted towards Lars and Hikari.

"What the-" Lars began.

The object landing on top of him and Hikari interrupted Lars. Lars, Hikari, and the object all groaned upon impact. The bartender shoved the object that was wrapped in material off of him and Lars before inspecting it further. Lars rubbed the back of his head where it had smacked against the stone ground. He withdrew his broadsword and slid off the material from the object.

"A priest?" Hikari raised an eyebrow, "Well, I guess we've found the church."

"Y'know, he's heavy for an old guy." Lars shook his head,

"Is he still breathing at least?"

Hikari put his ear to the unconscious priest's mouth and listened for any sounds of breathing. He heard a definite pattern and nodded to Lars. Lars slid his broadsword back in its scabbard and looked up through the now-exposed hole.

"Alright, let's get up top." Lars said. "Hikari, help me with this old guy, will you?"

Izlude quietly pulled himself onto the glossy, wooden floor of the Goddess' Church. He was immediately stared down by several religious paintings, which seemed to be throwing figurative daggers at him. He stared at them all with a slightly gaping mouth before helping Lars and Hikari.

Soon, the three of them were finally on ground level along with the unconscious priest. A thick, wooden door lay in front of them and was the only new way they could go. Lars and Hikari laid the priest down on a small couch in a corner of the room before silently approaching the wooden door. Lars placed a finger on his lips and pressed his ear against the oak. He could hear muffled grunts of protest and Mr. Kragon's familiar "Yup!"s. Lars grabbed his broadsword and prepared to open the door when Hikari stopped him.

"Wait!" he cautioned. "There could be more guards in there. We're going to have to go about this another way."

"He's got Marina in there!" Lars hissed. "We've got to go in there now!"

"He won't be marrying her any time soon with the priest out of commission," Hikari responded while gesturing to the comatose priest.

Lars put his hand on his chin and examined the priest from afar. Several moments later, he was dressed in the priest's robes, jewellery, and headpiece. He frowned as he adjusted the final item on his head.

"This hat's too big for me," Lars sighed, "and do these robes make me look a little overweight?"

"He's going to recognize you, Lars!" Hikari slapped a hand on his forehead.

"You guys just wait for the signal before rushing out, alright?" Lars ordered. "Do you remember what it is?"

"...I now pronounce you as husband and wife?" Hikari's eyebrows furled.

"Yeah!" Lars paused and shook his head, "No! By then it's too late! It's when I say, 'Should anyone object to these two being married, say so now or forever hold your peace.' I'll only say it if there are guards in there."

"R-Right..." Izlude said.

Lars took a deep breath, adjusted his priestly hat once more and walked through the door. He quickly scanned the room as he made his way to the altar for any guards but saw none.

"Yup, yup! I was right! You look younger too!" Mr. Kragon smiled goofily.

Lars stepped up behind the altar and cleared his voice. He caught Marina's eyes and gave her a hidden wink. Marina, realizing that it was Lars, became suddenly confused and worried. She knew Mr. Kragon wasn't the brightest of the bunch, but if he recognized Lars, it was game over. She tried to warn him through her gag, but only managed to make grunts.

"Where were we?" Lars mumbled, trying to hide his voice.

"You were just gonna marry us! Yup, yup!" Mr. Kragon grinned toothily.

"Was I now?" Lars mumbled, slowly reaching for his broadsword.

"You don't look like the priest." Mr. Kragon sniffed violently, "But you look kinda familiar, yup."

Lars suddenly whipped off the priestly garments and threw them to the ground. Mr. Kragon took a few steps back, but did not appear to be surprised. He pointed a solitary finger at Lars and scowled at him.

"You're the one who wants to steal Marina from me!" Mr. Kragon said. "You can't have her! We're in love! Yup, yup! She's mine!"

"Love? You call that love?!" Lars motioned to Marina on the floor, "You're nothing but a snot-nosed, immature moron!"

"That's not very nice to say on our wedding day." Mr.

Kragon sniffed again. "And I have allergies! Yup, yup. You're just jealous that Marina loves me instead of you! Well, we'll see about that! Xander! Marina and I are getting bored!"

"...Xander?" Lars blinked.

He hadn't seen anyone in the room when he had first entered. He quickly scanned it again. Lars watched as a muscle-clad figure lightly dropped from the rafters where it had been hiding. It walked over to Lars and stared him down. Xander was easily two feet taller than Lars. His head did not have a single trace of hair on it and tattered rags covered his bottom half.

"Well now, you're a big boy, aren't you?" Lars said as he looked up.

He made to unsheathe his broadsword but as soon as he pulled it out, Xander delivered a strong punch to Lars' chest. The blow sent him crashing backwards. The force of Lars' body slamming against the back wall jarred his thoughts and he let his broadsword fall to the ground with a clang.

"Should any king abject...No, that wasn't it..." Lars muttered while stunned, "Objectifying the carriage...no."

Xander chuckled and stepped over Marina on his way to Lars. Marina struggled furiously with her chains but sat helplessly as she watched Xander pick Lars up and hurl him in the opposite direction. Mr. Kragon had to duck as Lars passed by him. The pews in the front row stopped his path.

"Just come on out already!!" Lars shouted loudly at the wooden door.

Hikari and Izlude burst through the door to the priest's quarters, weapons drawn. Xander stared them down and began to approach them. Hikari looked around the room between Lars, Mr. Kragon, Marina, and the approaching behemoth in front of him. Lars was struggling to get up off of the ground and was very dazed.

"Izlude, you need to get to Marina and get her loose. I'll distract him." Hikari told Izlude quietly.

Hikari flipped his dagger around in his right hand so that the blade rested near his forearm and brought his hands up in front of him. Xander kept his same pace and eventually stood in front of the bartender. Hikari delivered a right hook with dagger in hand but Xander easily caught it. Hikari threw another punch with his left fist and groaned as he hit Xander's stomach muscles. The muscle-bound man seemed unaffected by the punch. Meanwhile, Lars had finally managed to stand himself up. He shook his head and took a step towards Mr. Kragon.

"Right." Lars assured himself but was immediately interrupted by Hikari crashing into him.

The two fell onto the broken pews and Lars was again dazed from the impact. Hikari was no better.

"Who invited you?" Lars groaned to the bartender.

It wasn't long before Xander dragged Izlude over to beside Lars and Hikari. Mr. Kragon grinned to his guard and patted him on the back. Xander smiled stupidly and stood in front of the altar. He placed the priest's hat on his head and looked down at the thick book in front of him with confusion. Mr. Kragon stood triumphantly over the three intruders.

"Yup, yup! See? Marina love me more!" Mr. Kragon grinned his toothy grin.

"What does that have anything to do with you owning a man made purely out of muscle?" Lars asked.

"He's half-giant! Yup!" Mr. Kragon giggled.

"Figures." Hikari groaned.

"I've decided to be nice! You're gonna be allowed to see our marriage!" Mr. Kragon nodded, "Aren't I nice, hunny?"

Marina shook her head with a look of disgust on her face. Mr. Kragon began walking back to the altar and took his place beside Marina. Xander picked up the book in front of them and flipped it around every way he could think of before throwing it behind him.

"She do?" Xander asked in a deep voice.

"Yup, yup!" Mr. Kragon answered, despite Marina's indecipherable protests.

"He do?" asked Xander.

Lars shook his head in defeat and looked at Marina. He silently apologized for failing and watched as Mr. Kragon adjusted himself before opening his mouth to respond.

"I-"

The thick, wooden door to the priest's quarters flung open and the priest, looking extremely frantic, ran inside, interrupting Mr. Kragon. Mr. Kragon was not impressed.

"Our wedding is being interrupted again!" Mr. Kragon scowled at the priest, "You look even worse now, yup."

"T-There's something beneath the church! I-It tried to grab me!!" the priest stammered, looking white as a ghost.

Lars, Hikari, and Izlude looked at each other with wide eyes.

Nah...it couldn't be that. The roof would've killed it, right? Lars thought to himself.

Mr. Kragon looked at Xander and pointed for him to investigate. Xander nodded several times before approaching the closed wooden door.

"Uh, Xander? I wouldn't do that." Lars cautioned.

"Xander! He's trying to trick you, yup. Open the door!" Mr. Kragon ordered.

Xander looked from Lars to Mr. Kragon before flinging the door open. He was welcomed by a single, blue slime arm that was protruding from the hole in the floor where the trapdoor had been. It shot forward and latched onto the half-giant and tried to pull him towards its main body.

Lars got up and sprinted past the altar for his broadsword. He shoulder-checked Mr. Kragon out of the way and grabbed onto the Arcanian artifact. Xander was desperately holding onto the doorframe with both hands. Lars ran as fast as he could and reached the arm just as Xander lost his grip. Lars quickly separated the arm with a slash from his broadsword and Xander was free. The two of them ran out of the room and slammed the wooden door shut.

"I can't believe that thing is still alive." Lars panted.

Xander extended both of his arms, grabbed Lars by the shoulders and lifted him up.

"Uh, oh." Lars blinked.

Xander pulled Lars into him for a bear hug and swung him left and right. Lars felt as if his bones were being ground to dust and groaned from the unending grasp of the half-giant.

"Put me down!" Lars protested. "You're welcome!"

"Sorry." Xander said sadly as he placed Lars back on the floor. "Xander alive! Xander pay small man back!"

"Small?!" Lars coughed, "If you want to pay me back, you could leave."

"Leave? Small man no want Xander here!" Xander began to cry loudly.

"N-No! It's not like that!" Lars took a step back, "We just have some business to take care of with Mr. Kragon."

"Oh." the half-giant replied. "Okay. Xander go."

Xander patted Lars on the head with one of his meaty fists, nearly knocking him out. Hikari and Izlude looked at each other as Xander walked towards the church doors. Mr. Kragon ran behind him to catch up.

"Where are you going, Xander?" Mr. Kragon asked the half-giant. "I give you money!"

"But small man say Xander can go!" Xander said with confusion.

"I don't care what 'small man say'!" Mr. Kragon shouted. "You're not my guard anymore if you leave, yup!"

"Xander go." Xander repeated as he walked through the church doors, leaving Mr. Kragon behind.

Mr. Kragon sniffed violently before turning around. Hikari, Lars, and Izlude greeted him. All three had their weapons drawn.

CHAPTER 25

"Now wait a minute!" Mr. Kragon said. "Marina and I just want to be married, yup!"

Lars had managed to back Mr. Kragon up into a corner and was brandishing his broadsword at him. Hikari had since removed Marina's gag but was struggling with her chains. Marina was royally ticked off.

"Married?!" Marina shouted from in front of the altar. "I don't even want to breathe the same air as you!"

"B-But how will we live happily ever after if we're not married?" Mr. Kragon sniffed.

"I can't get these chains off of Marina, Lars. They're held together by a padlock, he must have the key on him." Hikari said.

"A key, eh?" Lars said.

He walked up to Mr. Kragon and pressed him against the wall. Lars felt something in the pocket of his multi-coloured suit jacket and slipped his hand in. He removed two objects, one a key and the other a silver stone. He pocketed the stone in his right pocket and tossed the key in the air before catching it. Lars let Mr. Kragon fall to the ground and turned to face Hikari and Marina.

"Yeah, I found the key." Lars nodded as he tossed the key to Hikari.

Hikari and Marina weren't interested in the key at the moment, however. They were more interested in the fact that Lars' right pocket was glowing. Hikari caught the key as Lars tossed it to him without taking his eyes off Lars' pocket. Lars raised an eyebrow and waved to get their attention.

"Uh, hello?" he said.

"Bro...y-your pants..." Izlude finally spoke, "They're glowing..."

"What?" Lars looked down.

He jumped back in surprise before stuffing his hand into his pocket and withdrawing the orb map he had found on the pirate sky ship. It immediately stopped glowing once it reached his face. Lars frowned and went to place it back in his pocket but stopped as it began to glow once more. With his other hand, Lars withdrew the silver stone he had just taken from Mr. Kragon and moved it various distances from the orb in his right hand.

"It's a map piece..." Marina stated in shock.

Hikari snapped out of being mesmerized and quickly unlocked Marina from her chains. She stood up, rubbed her wrists, and walked up to Lars.

"I can't believe it." Marina said. "All this time, this idiot had it?"

"Give me back my family heirloom!" Mr. Kragon protested. "It was given to me by my father, yup, yup!"

"How do we attach it?" Lars ignored Mr. Kragon.

"I...I don't know, Lars!" Marina replied.

Lars tapped the silver stone against the orb and nearly dropped it when the stone was pulled inside. The map orb began to vibrate and hum loudly before a large explosion of light filled the room. The map was being projected onto the walls again. Lars looked around the church walls for anything that had been changed in the map and it wasn't before long that he found a large green triangle placed over top of Port Tasuna.

"Marina! Over there!" Lars shouted while pointing at it.

For a short while, all that had been altered was the green triangle. Just as Lars was thinking that it was possible that the green triangle was all they would see, a dotted path slowly scrawled itself towards what seemed like a rectangular building outside of town. The words "Tekky's Tower" revealed themselves beneath it.

"Aha! I knew it!" Lars cheered. "That's the next piece!"

"Thank you, Lars." Marina said as she embraced him.

"O-Oh, uh..." Lars blushed slightly, "It was nothing, really."

"You still came for me, even though you didn't have to." Marina smiled.

"Are you sure you don't want to come with us?" Lars asked her.

"Marina! If you leave this church and we're not going on our honeymoon, you can't go on any more adventures!" Mr. Kragon threatened, "I'm kicking you out of my Treasure Hunters Society! Yup! And Captain Cyrus is gonna lose his ship!"

"I can't go with you, Lars..." Marina let Lars go and lowered her head.

"What?" Lars said, taken aback. "You're letting him win? You can't stop people from going on adventures, Marina! This moron here thinks that he can control them! Well you know what? He can't! Did Izlude, Hikari, and I pay for the adventure we had getting here? Heck no! We didn't do it for sandwiches or the prospect of treasure! It's not an adventure if everything is planned, Marina! You need to stand up to this snot-nosed bastard and tell him he doesn't own you! I promise, Marina, we'll find your sister and the Crystal of Immortality."

Silence filled the room. Izlude shuffled uncomfortably where he stood, Hikari nodded in silent agreement with what Lars had said, and Mr. Kragon scowled in the corner. Marina smiled to herself before looking Mr. Kragon straight in the eye.

"He's right. You don't own me." Marina said to him. "Go ahead! Kick me out of your stupid Treasure Hunters Society! I'm going treasure hunting wherever I want, whenever I want! And if you dare to take Captain Cyrus' ship from him... I'll make sure that Lars here personally has a little 'chat' with you."

Mr. Kragon's face drained of blood and for the first time, he had nothing to say. Lars nodded to Marina and grinned. She smiled back at him with her usual glow about her. That done, Lars, Marina, Hikari, and Izlude walked out of the Goddess' Church.

The sunlight caused Lars to shade his eyes for a few seconds before he adapted. Loud firecrackers erupted and confetti was thrown all around them. A hundred people were standing outside the church gates clapping and cheering, the guards who were previously guarding the entrance among them.

"Congratulations on the marriage, Mr. Kragon!" shouted a man.

"But that doesn't look like Mr. Kragon..." responded a woman.

"Who cares?!" roared another man. "It's party time!!"

"No! We're not married!" Marina protested. "It's a misunderstanding!"

But no one listened. The crowd had already run off into the streets to officially start the post-wedding, citywide party. Hikari scratched the back of his head before looking at Izlude and shrugging with him. Marina sighed and began to rip off her wedding gown, eventually revealing her treasure-hunting outfit beneath it.

"They actually think we're married!" Lars laughed. "Let's milk it the most we can, we could all use a day off."

"Lars, I've had enough adventure for a lifetime. I'm going to head back to the Sky Princess." Hikari suddenly said.

"You're not coming with us, Hikari?" Lars asked the bartender.

"Sorry, Lars. I've heard enough stories about the Crystal of Immortality to know that I wouldn't be of any help to you. Besides, I have another year left on my contract with Captain Cyrus before I can leave." Hikari explained.

"Alright. Take care, okay?" Lars nodded to him. "And thanks."

"Yeah, no sweat!" Hikari replied with a wave as he ran off into the crowd.

"Heh, let's hit the town!" Lars cheered triumphantly.

He ran through the church gates with Marina at his side and Izlude close behind them. The port town was filled with joyful music, flowing alcohol, and numerous games. Lars was certain that the only unhappy person in the entire city was Mr. Kragon. He shook his head with a roguish grin on his face. He wouldn't think about that sorry excuse for a man. This was the start of his adventure and he was going to enjoy every moment of it that he could.

CHAPTER 26

Three people occupied the dark office. Various flags flaunting the Lucarian insignia adorned the walls. A desk separated the two standing men from another who was seated in an ornate chair, its back facing the two others. One of the men on the other side of the desk dressed head to toe in black platemail broke the silence.

"My liege, are you certain that this...pathetic man can be trusted?" his voice growled.

"Yes, dark knight. While his mental capacities are questionable, what he described to me could be none other than the Arcanian artifact we have been searching for." responded the high-ranking man in the chair.

"What would you have us do?" asked a younger voice, coming from the smaller man beside the dark knight.

"You need to ask, Peacemaker Trayze? You may have only just reached the ranks of peacemaker, but you won't progress much further if you don't think," hissed the man in the chair. "Our main troops are busy fighting the war against those rebel bastards in Morjan. The two of you will take your squads, proceed to Port Tasuna, and take the map to the Crystal of Immortality. If force is required, then so be it."

"Yes, sir." the two men responded before taking their leave.

"Heh, heh, heh. Lars Nokuten, was it? Very interesting." the man in the chair mused.